NANCY DREW

girl detective ®

PAPERCUT<u>Z</u> ™

NANCY DREW

girl detective®

Graphic Novels
Available from Papercutz

#1 The Demon of River Heights
#2 Writ In Stone
#3 The Haunted Dollhouse
#4 The Girl Who Wasn't There
#5 The Fake Heir (coming May 2006)

$7.95 each in paperback
$12.95 each in hardcover

Please add $3.00 for postage and handling for the first book, add $1.00 for each additional book.

Send for our catalog:
Papercutz
555 Eighth Avenue, Suite 1202
New York, NY 10018
www.papercutz.com

NANCY
DREW
girl detective
#1
BASED ON THE SERIES BY CAROLYN KEENE
PAPERCUTZ

NANCY
DREW
girl detective
#2
BASED ON THE SERIES BY CAROLYN KEENE
PAPERCUTZ

ALL-NEW STORY FULL-COLOR GRAPHIC NOVEL
NANCY
DREW
girl detective
#3
BASED ON THE SERIES BY CAROLYN KEENE
Stefan PETRUCHA
Sho MURASE
PAPERCUTZ

NANCY
DREW
girl detective
#4
BASED ON THE SERIES BY CAROLYN KEENE
PAPERCUTZ

NANCY
DREW
girl detective
#5
BASED ON THE SERIES BY CAROLYN KEENE
PAPERCUTZ

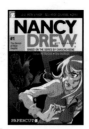

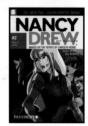

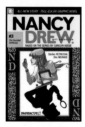

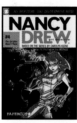

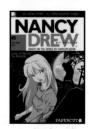

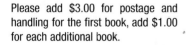

NANCY DREW
girl detective ®

#4

The Girl Who Wasn't There

STEFAN PETRUCHA • Writer
SHO MURASE • Artist
with 3D CG elements by RACHEL ITO
preview art by VAUGHN ROSS
Based on the series by
CAROLYN KEENE

New York

The Girl Who Wasn't There
STEFAN PETRUCHA – Writer
SHO MURASE – Artist
with 3D CG elements by RACHEL ITO
BRYAN SENKA – Letterer
CARLOS JOSE GUZMAN
SHO MURASE
Colorists
JIM SALICRUP
Editor-in-Chief

ISBN 10: 1-59707-012-2 paperback edition
ISBN 13: 978-1-59707-012-6 paperback edition
ISBN 10: 1-59707-013-0 hardcover edition
ISBN 13: 978-1-59707-013-3 hardcover edition

Printed in China.

10 9 8 7 6 5 4 3 2 1

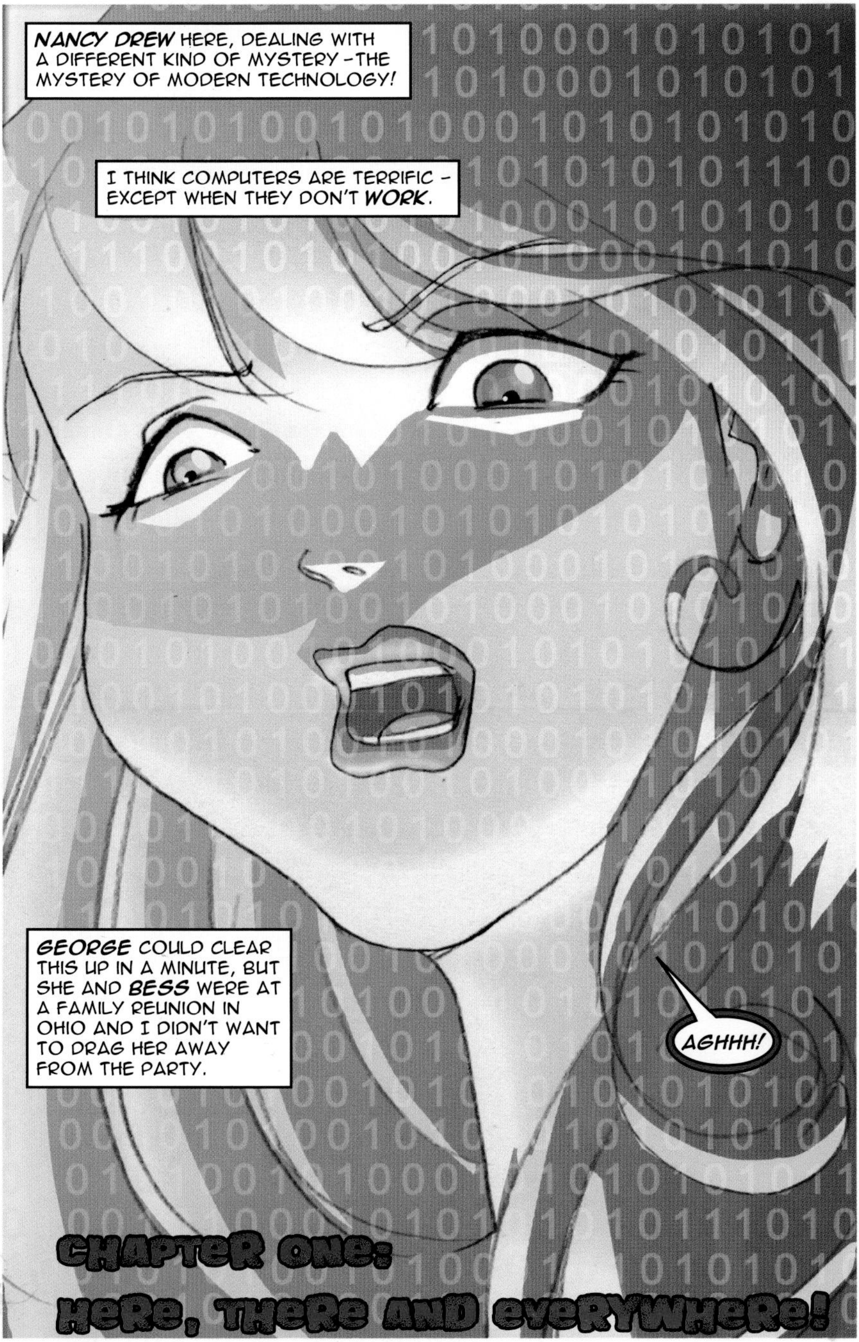
NANCY DREW HERE, DEALING WITH A DIFFERENT KIND OF MYSTERY –THE MYSTERY OF MODERN TECHNOLOGY!
I THINK COMPUTERS ARE TERRIFIC – EXCEPT WHEN THEY DON'T WORK.
GEORGE COULD CLEAR THIS UP IN A MINUTE, BUT SHE AND BESS WERE AT A FAMILY REUNION IN OHIO AND I DIDN'T WANT TO DRAG HER AWAY FROM THE PARTY.
AGHHH!
CHAPTER ONE:
HERE, THERE AND EVERYWHERE!

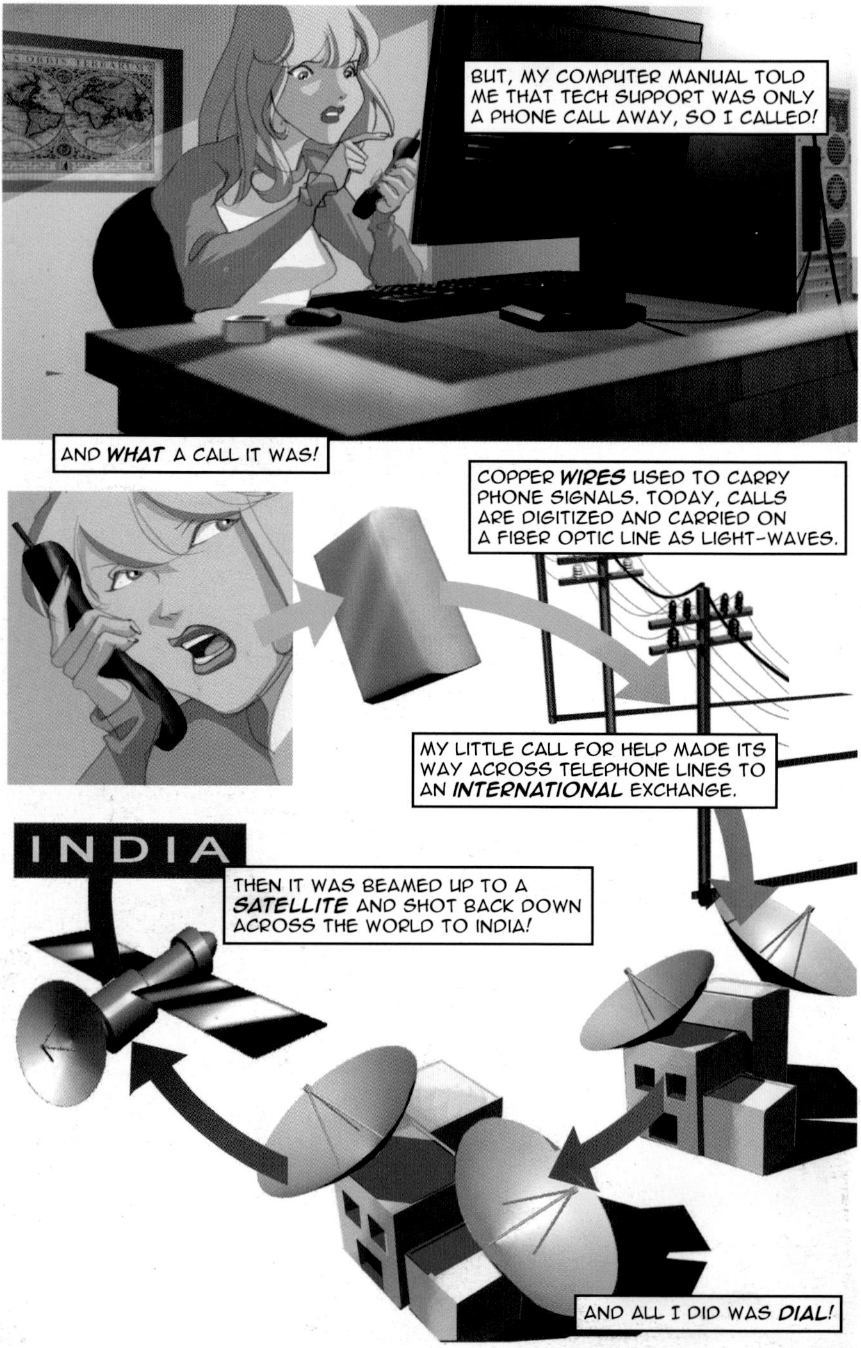
BUT, MY COMPUTER MANUAL TOLD ME THAT TECH SUPPORT WAS ONLY A PHONE CALL AWAY, SO I CALLED!
AND *WHAT* A CALL IT WAS!
COPPER *WIRES* USED TO CARRY PHONE SIGNALS. TODAY, CALLS ARE DIGITIZED AND CARRIED ON A FIBER OPTIC LINE AS LIGHT-WAVES.
MY LITTLE CALL FOR HELP MADE ITS WAY ACROSS TELEPHONE LINES TO AN *INTERNATIONAL* EXCHANGE.
INDIA
THEN IT WAS BEAMED UP TO A *SATELLITE* AND SHOT BACK DOWN ACROSS THE WORLD TO INDIA!
AND ALL I DID WAS *DIAL*!

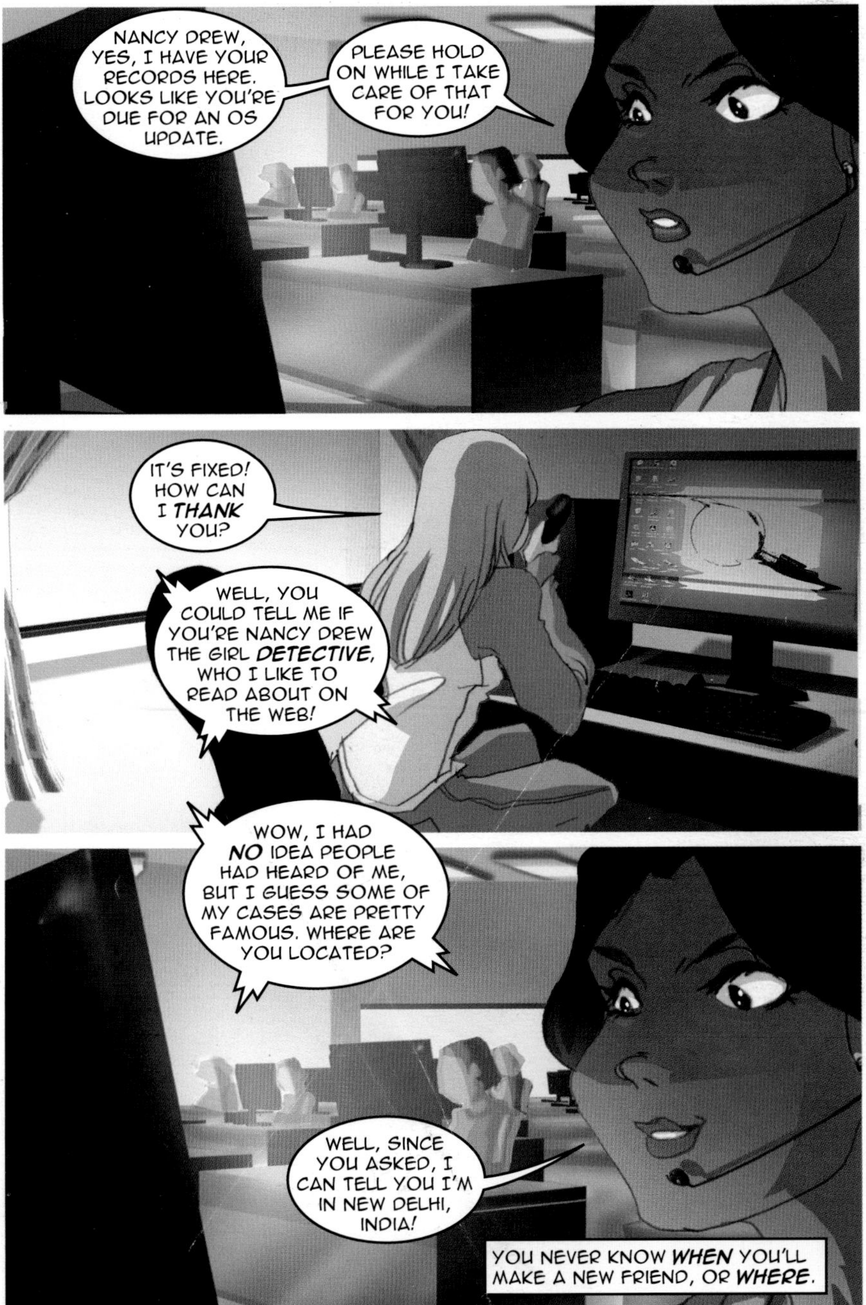
NANCY DREW, YES, I HAVE YOUR RECORDS HERE. LOOKS LIKE YOU'RE DUE FOR AN OS UPDATE.
PLEASE HOLD ON WHILE I TAKE CARE OF THAT FOR YOU!
IT'S FIXED! HOW CAN I *THANK* YOU?
WELL, YOU COULD TELL ME IF YOU'RE NANCY DREW THE GIRL *DETECTIVE*, WHO I LIKE TO READ ABOUT ON THE WEB!
WOW, I HAD **NO** IDEA PEOPLE HAD HEARD OF ME, BUT I GUESS SOME OF MY CASES ARE PRETTY FAMOUS. WHERE ARE YOU LOCATED?
WELL, SINCE YOU ASKED, I CAN TELL YOU I'M IN NEW DELHI, INDIA!
YOU NEVER KNOW ***WHEN*** YOU'LL MAKE A NEW FRIEND, OR ***WHERE***.

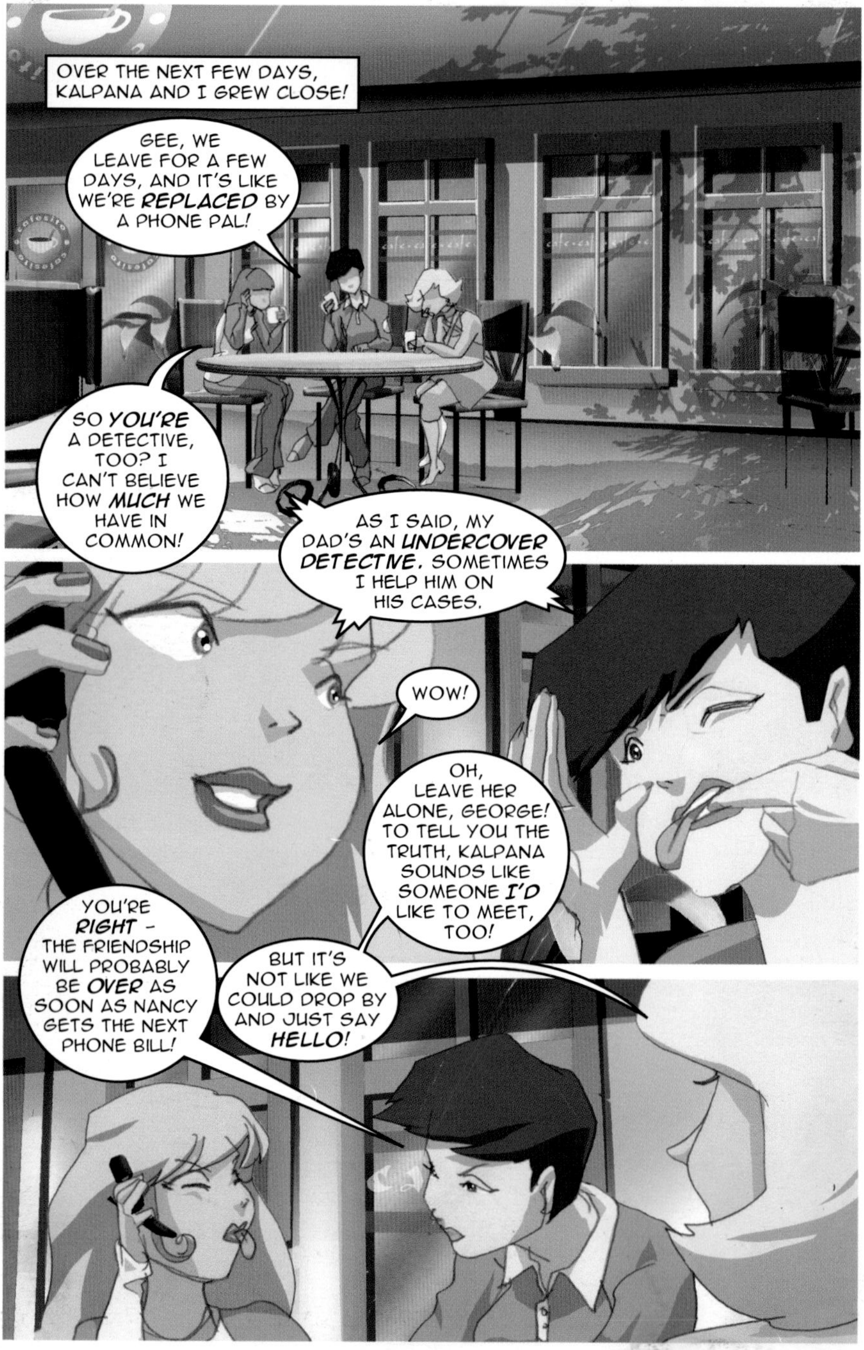
OVER THE NEXT FEW DAYS, KALPANA AND I GREW CLOSE!
GEE, WE LEAVE FOR A FEW DAYS, AND IT'S LIKE WE'RE *REPLACED* BY A PHONE PAL!
SO *YOU'RE* A DETECTIVE, TOO? I CAN'T BELIEVE HOW *MUCH* WE HAVE IN COMMON!
AS I SAID, MY DAD'S AN *UNDERCOVER DETECTIVE.* SOMETIMES I HELP HIM ON HIS CASES.
WOW!
OH, LEAVE HER ALONE, GEORGE! TO TELL YOU THE TRUTH, KALPANA SOUNDS LIKE SOMEONE *I'D* LIKE TO MEET, TOO!
YOU'RE *RIGHT* – THE FRIENDSHIP WILL PROBABLY BE *OVER* AS SOON AS NANCY GETS THE NEXT PHONE BILL!
BUT IT'S NOT LIKE WE COULD DROP BY AND JUST SAY *HELLO*!

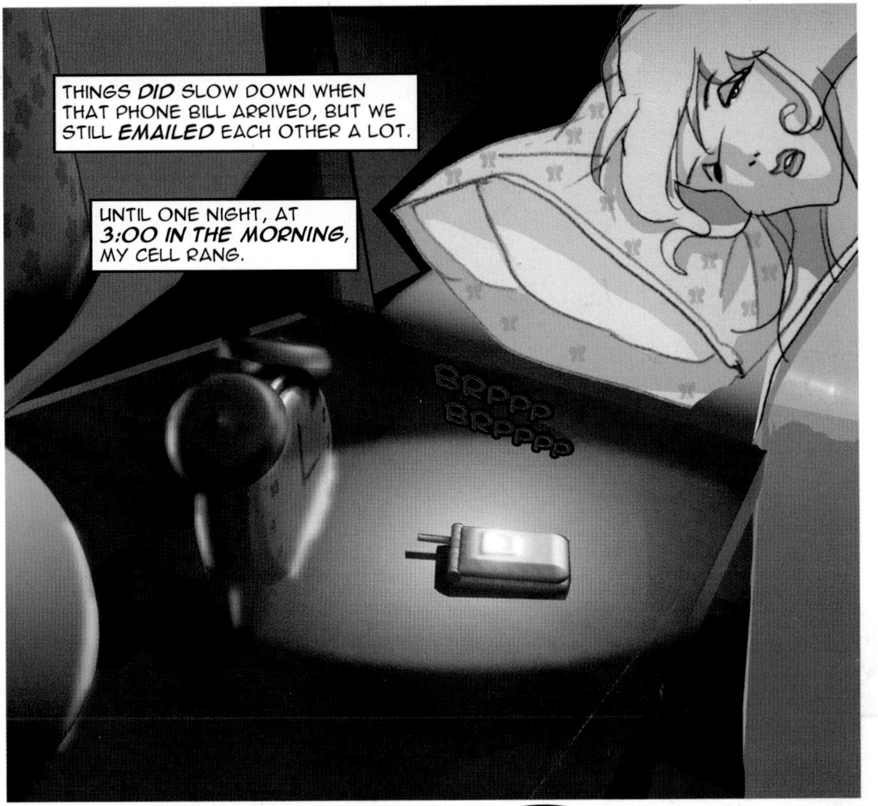
THINGS DID SLOW DOWN WHEN THAT PHONE BILL ARRIVED, BUT WE STILL EMAILED EACH OTHER A LOT.
UNTIL ONE NIGHT, AT 3:00 IN THE MORNING, MY CELL RANG.
BRPPPP BRPPPPP

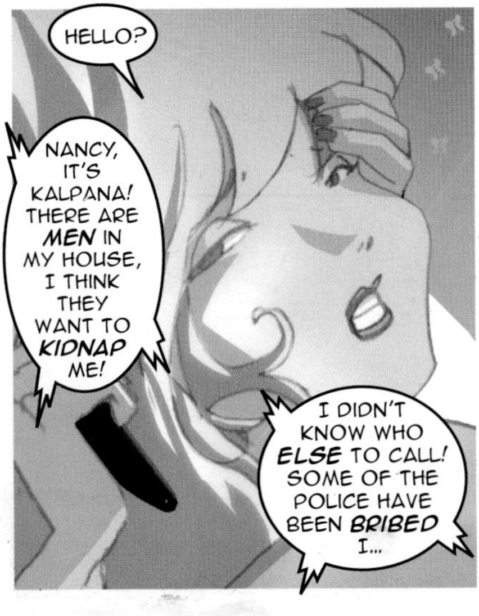
HELLO?
NANCY, IT'S KALPANA! THERE ARE MEN IN MY HOUSE, I THINK THEY WANT TO KIDNAP ME!
I DIDN'T KNOW WHO ELSE TO CALL! SOME OF THE POLICE HAVE BEEN BRIBED I...

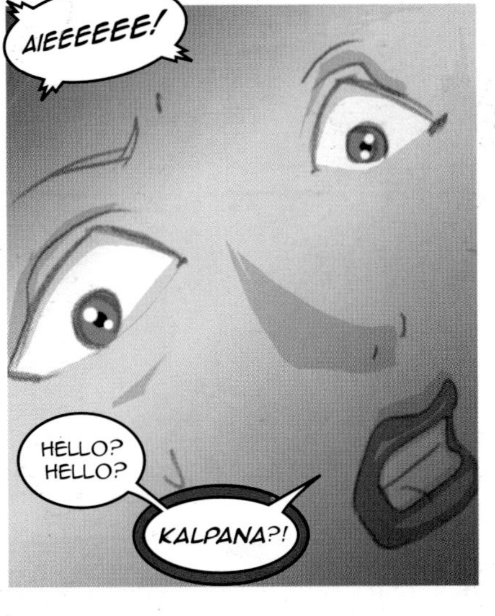
AIEEEEEE!
HELLO? HELLO?
KALPANA?!

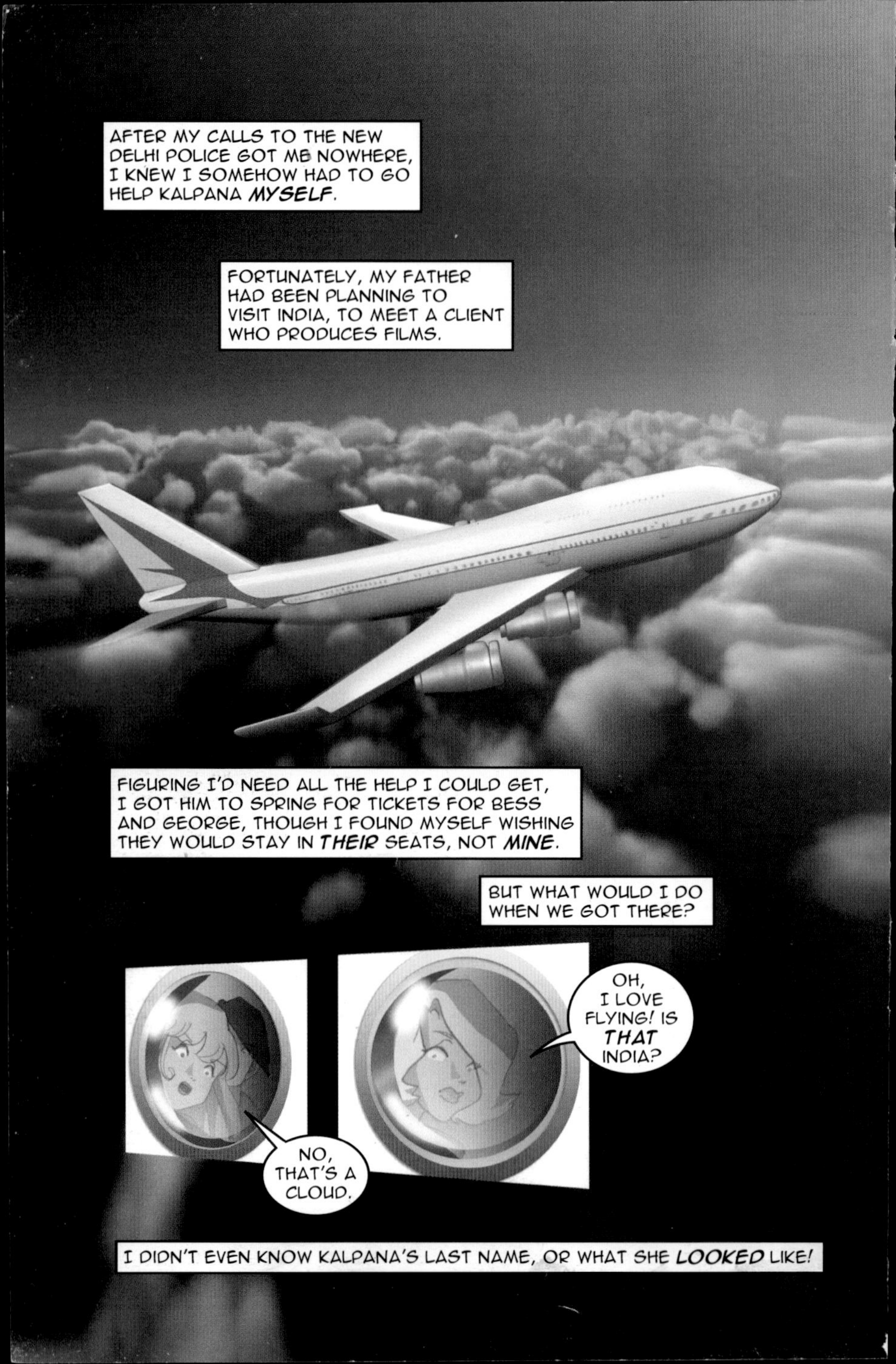
AFTER MY CALLS TO THE NEW DELHI POLICE GOT ME NOWHERE, I KNEW I SOMEHOW HAD TO GO HELP KALPANA MYSELF.
FORTUNATELY, MY FATHER HAD BEEN PLANNING TO VISIT INDIA, TO MEET A CLIENT WHO PRODUCES FILMS.
FIGURING I'D NEED ALL THE HELP I COULD GET, I GOT HIM TO SPRING FOR TICKETS FOR BESS AND GEORGE, THOUGH I FOUND MYSELF WISHING THEY WOULD STAY IN THEIR SEATS, NOT MINE.
BUT WHAT WOULD I DO WHEN WE GOT THERE?
OH, I LOVE FLYING! IS THAT INDIA?
NO, THAT'S A CLOUD.
I DIDN'T EVEN KNOW KALPANA'S LAST NAME, OR WHAT SHE LOOKED LIKE!

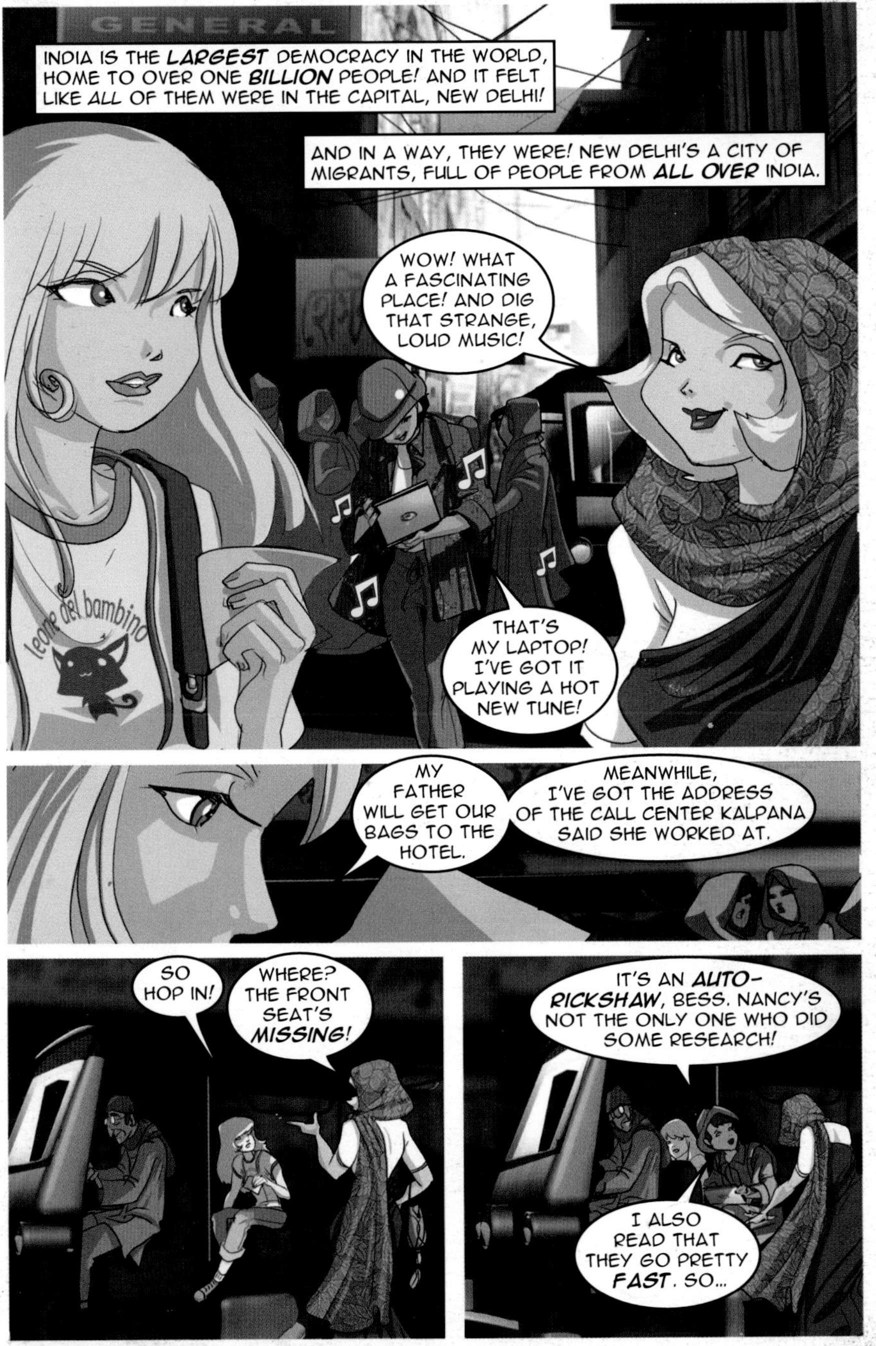
GENERAL
INDIA IS THE *LARGEST* DEMOCRACY IN THE WORLD, HOME TO OVER ONE *BILLION* PEOPLE! AND IT FELT LIKE *ALL* OF THEM WERE IN THE CAPITAL, NEW DELHI!
AND IN A WAY, THEY WERE! NEW DELHI'S A CITY OF MIGRANTS, FULL OF PEOPLE FROM *ALL OVER* INDIA.
WOW! WHAT A FASCINATING PLACE! AND DIG THAT STRANGE, LOUD MUSIC!
THAT'S MY LAPTOP! I'VE GOT IT PLAYING A HOT NEW TUNE!
leone del bambino
MY FATHER WILL GET OUR BAGS TO THE HOTEL.
MEANWHILE, I'VE GOT THE ADDRESS OF THE CALL CENTER KALPANA SAID SHE WORKED AT.
SO HOP IN!
WHERE? THE FRONT SEAT'S *MISSING*!
IT'S AN *AUTO-RICKSHAW*, BESS. NANCY'S NOT THE ONLY ONE WHO DID SOME RESEARCH!
I ALSO READ THAT THEY GO PRETTY *FAST*. SO...

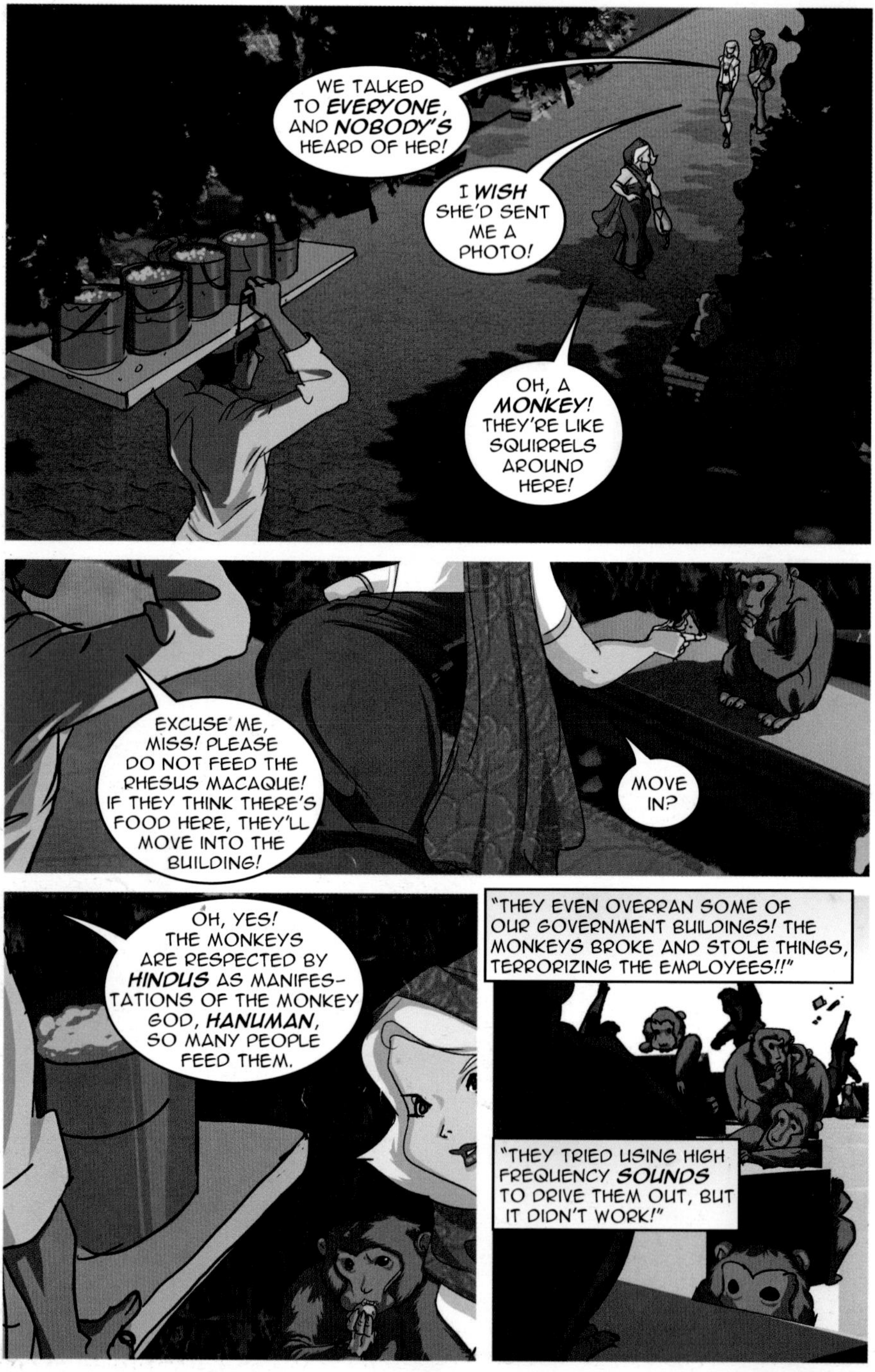
WE TALKED TO EVERYONE, AND NOBODY'S HEARD OF HER!
I WISH SHE'D SENT ME A PHOTO!
OH, A MONKEY! THEY'RE LIKE SQUIRRELS AROUND HERE!
EXCUSE ME, MISS! PLEASE DO NOT FEED THE RHESUS MACAQUE! IF THEY THINK THERE'S FOOD HERE, THEY'LL MOVE INTO THE BUILDING!
MOVE IN?
OH, YES! THE MONKEYS ARE RESPECTED BY HINDUS AS MANIFESTATIONS OF THE MONKEY GOD, HANUMAN, SO MANY PEOPLE FEED THEM.
"THEY EVEN OVERRAN SOME OF OUR GOVERNMENT BUILDINGS! THE MONKEYS BROKE AND STOLE THINGS, TERRORIZING THE EMPLOYEES!!"
"THEY TRIED USING HIGH FREQUENCY SOUNDS TO DRIVE THEM OUT, BUT IT DIDN'T WORK!"

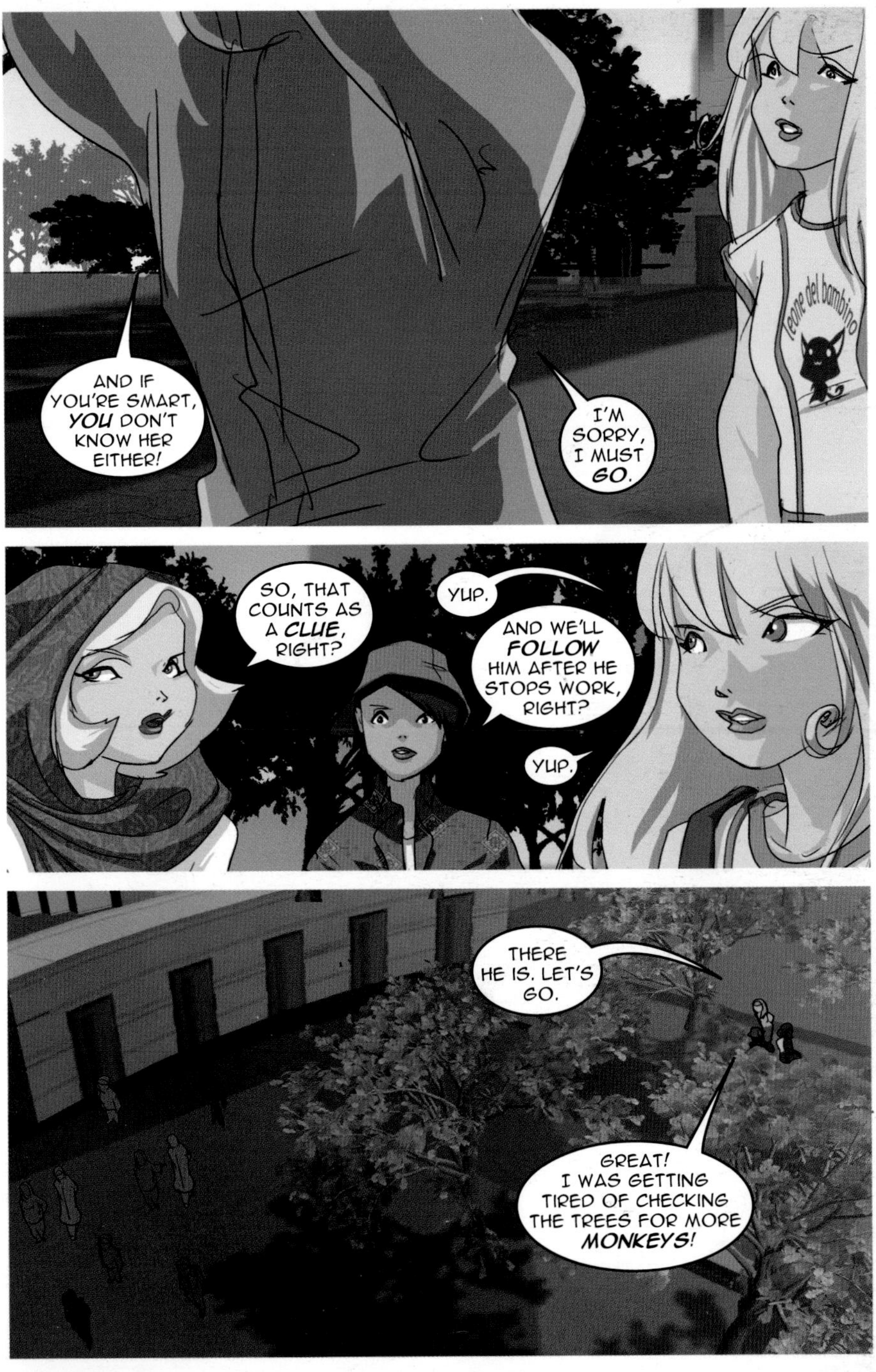
AND IF YOU'RE SMART, *YOU* DON'T KNOW HER EITHER!
I'M SORRY, I MUST *GO*.
SO, THAT COUNTS AS A *CLUE*, RIGHT?
YUP.
AND WE'LL *FOLLOW* HIM AFTER HE STOPS WORK, RIGHT?
YUP.
THERE HE IS. LET'S GO.
GREAT! I WAS GETTING TIRED OF CHECKING THE TREES FOR MORE *MONKEYS*!
teone del bambino

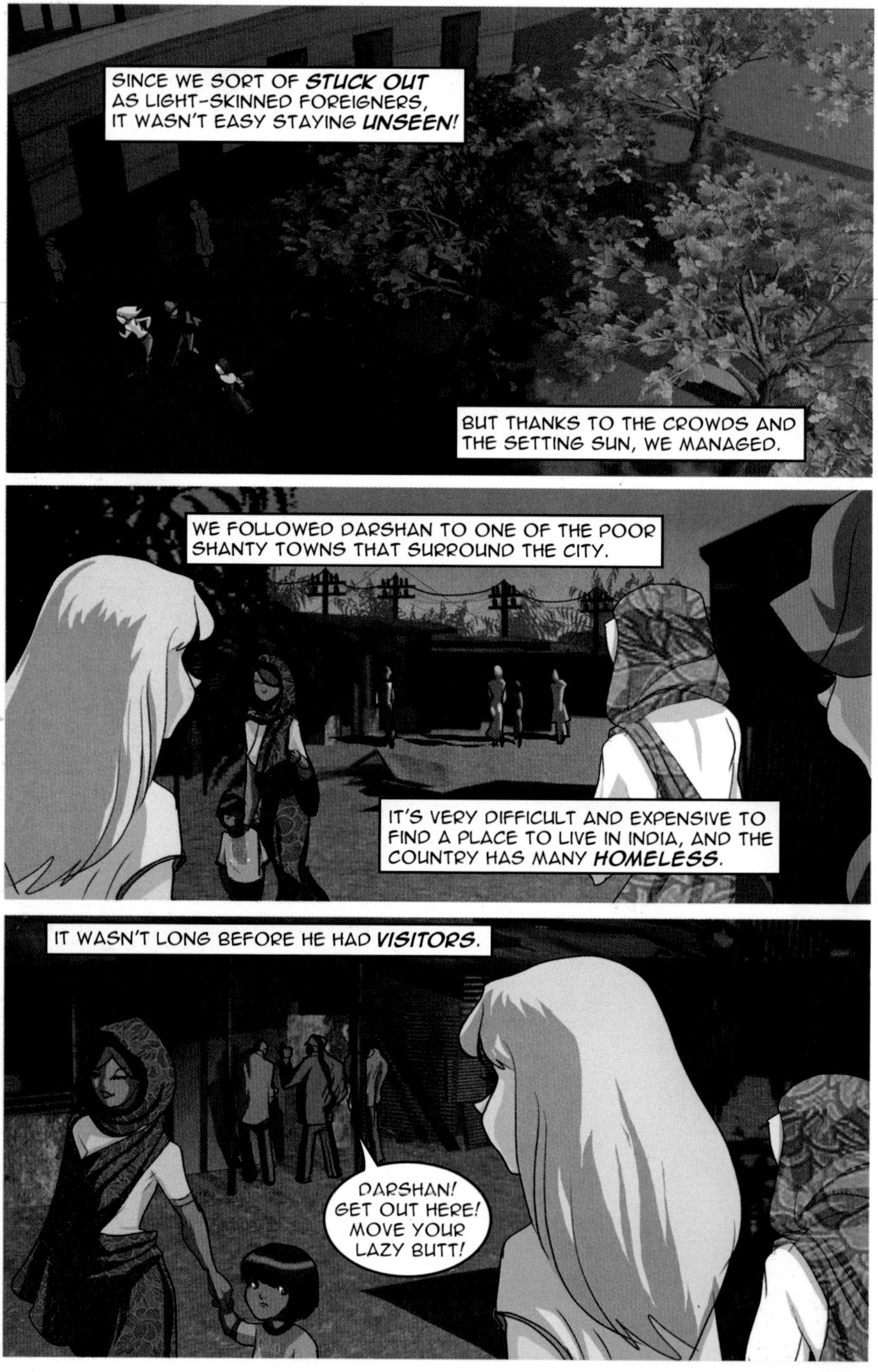
SINCE WE SORT OF STUCK OUT AS LIGHT-SKINNED FOREIGNERS, IT WASN'T EASY STAYING UNSEEN!
BUT THANKS TO THE CROWDS AND THE SETTING SUN, WE MANAGED.
WE FOLLOWED DARSHAN TO ONE OF THE POOR SHANTY TOWNS THAT SURROUND THE CITY.
IT'S VERY DIFFICULT AND EXPENSIVE TO FIND A PLACE TO LIVE IN INDIA, AND THE COUNTRY HAS MANY HOMELESS.
IT WASN'T LONG BEFORE HE HAD VISITORS.
DARSHAN! GET OUT HERE! MOVE YOUR LAZY BUTT!

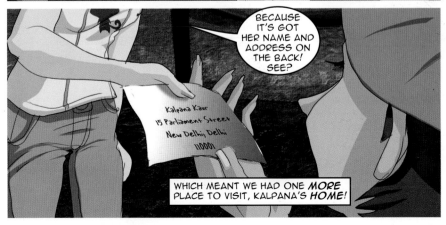

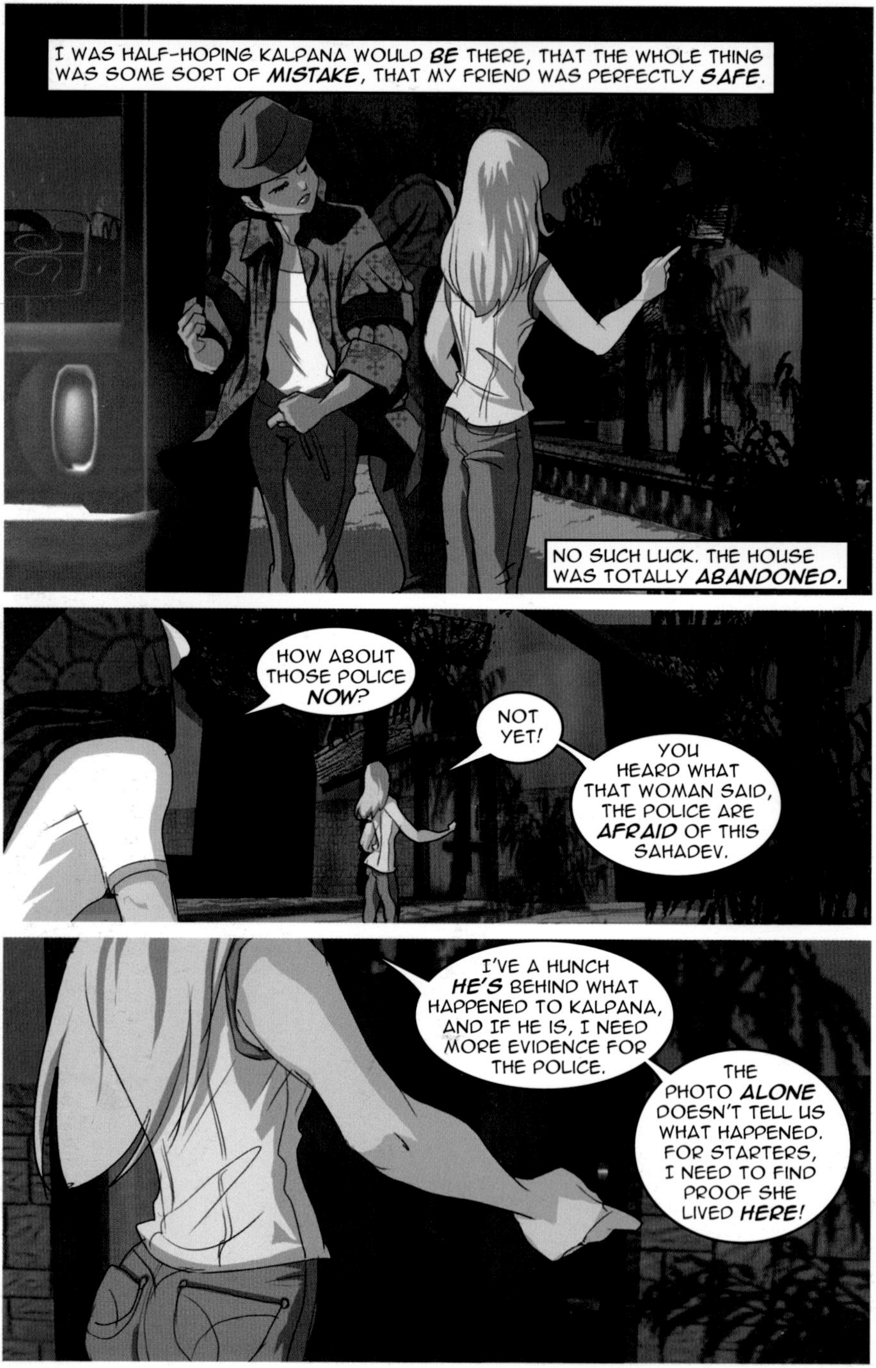
I WAS HALF-HOPING KALPANA WOULD BE THERE, THAT THE WHOLE THING WAS SOME SORT OF MISTAKE, THAT MY FRIEND WAS PERFECTLY SAFE.
NO SUCH LUCK. THE HOUSE WAS TOTALLY ABANDONED.
HOW ABOUT THOSE POLICE NOW?
NOT YET!
YOU HEARD WHAT THAT WOMAN SAID, THE POLICE ARE AFRAID OF THIS SAHADEV.
I'VE A HUNCH HE'S BEHIND WHAT HAPPENED TO KALPANA, AND IF HE IS, I NEED MORE EVIDENCE FOR THE POLICE.
THE PHOTO ALONE DOESN'T TELL US WHAT HAPPENED. FOR STARTERS, I NEED TO FIND PROOF SHE LIVED HERE!

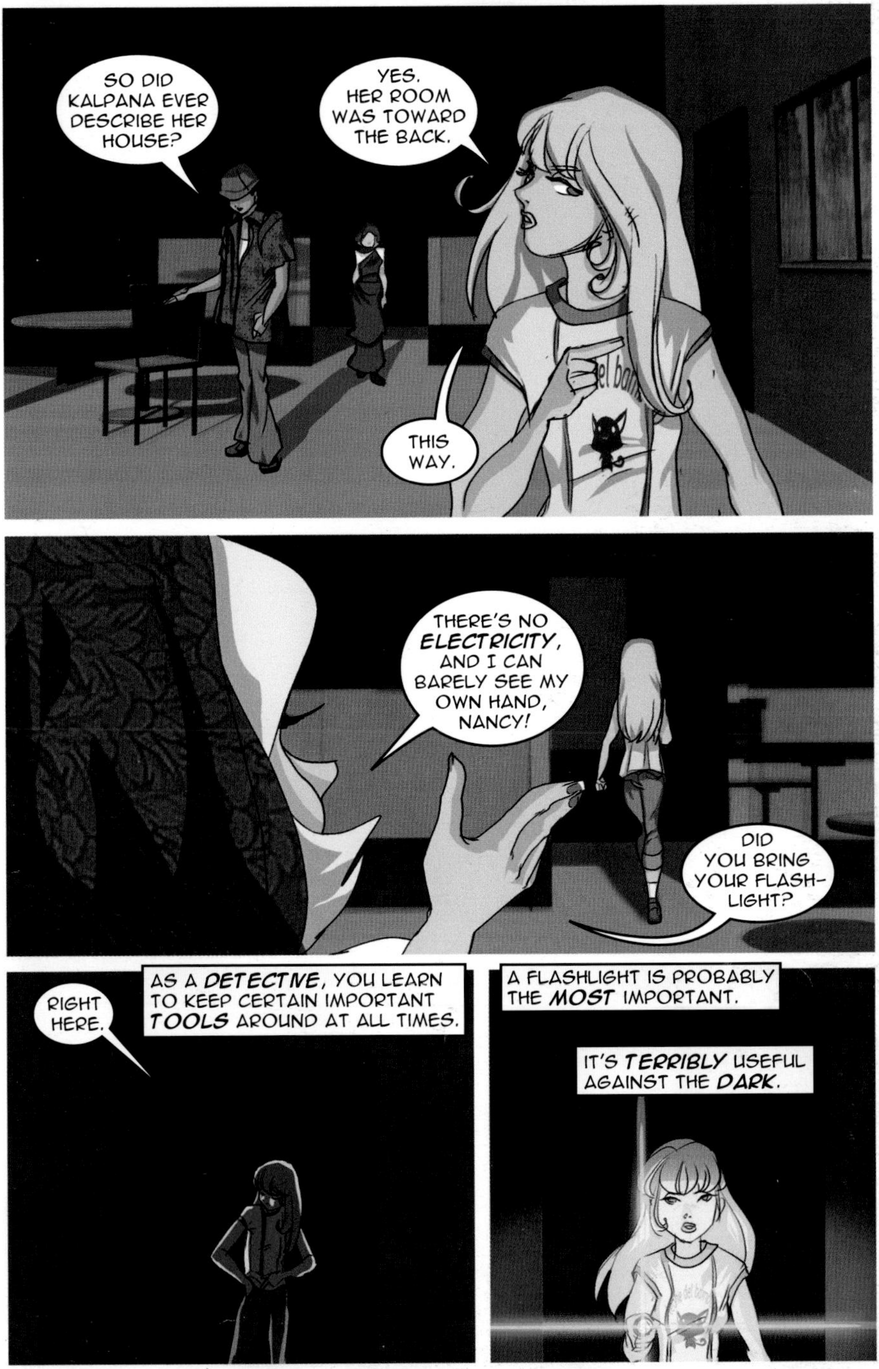
SO DID KALPANA EVER DESCRIBE HER HOUSE?
YES. HER ROOM WAS TOWARD THE BACK.
THIS WAY.
THERE'S NO *ELECTRICITY*, AND I CAN BARELY SEE MY OWN HAND, NANCY!
DID YOU BRING YOUR FLASH-LIGHT?
RIGHT HERE.
AS A *DETECTIVE*, YOU LEARN TO KEEP CERTAIN IMPORTANT *TOOLS* AROUND AT ALL TIMES.
A FLASHLIGHT IS PROBABLY THE *MOST* IMPORTANT.
IT'S *TERRIBLY* USEFUL AGAINST THE *DARK*.

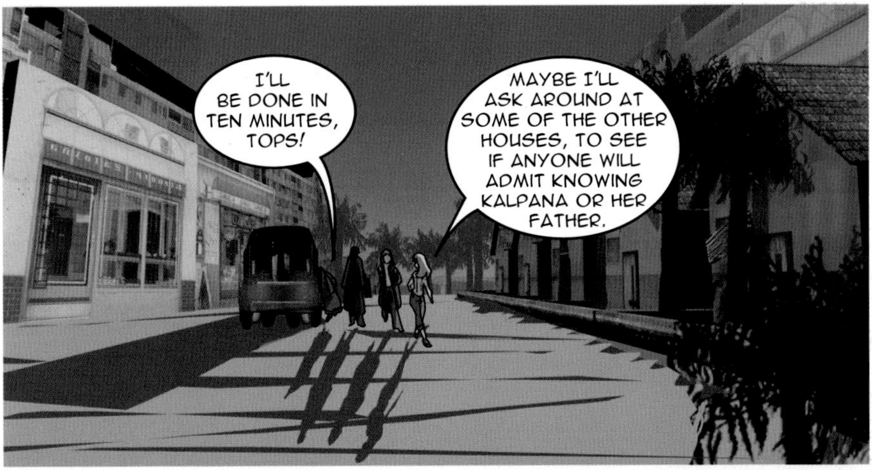
I'LL BE DONE IN TEN MINUTES, TOPS!
MAYBE I'LL ASK AROUND AT SOME OF THE OTHER HOUSES, TO SEE IF ANYONE WILL ADMIT KNOWING KALPANA OR HER FATHER.

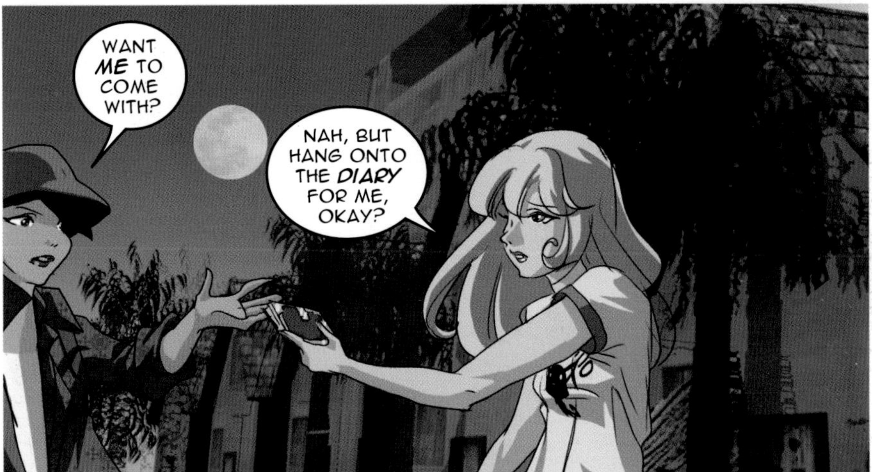
WANT *ME* TO COME WITH?
NAH, BUT HANG ONTO THE *DIARY* FOR ME, OKAY?

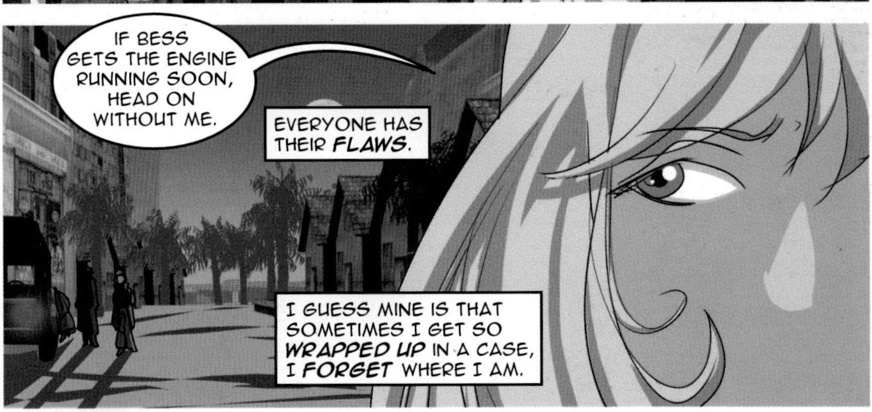
IF BESS GETS THE ENGINE RUNNING SOON, HEAD ON WITHOUT ME.
EVERYONE HAS THEIR *FLAWS*.
I GUESS MINE IS THAT SOMETIMES I GET SO *WRAPPED UP* IN A CASE, I *FORGET* WHERE I AM.

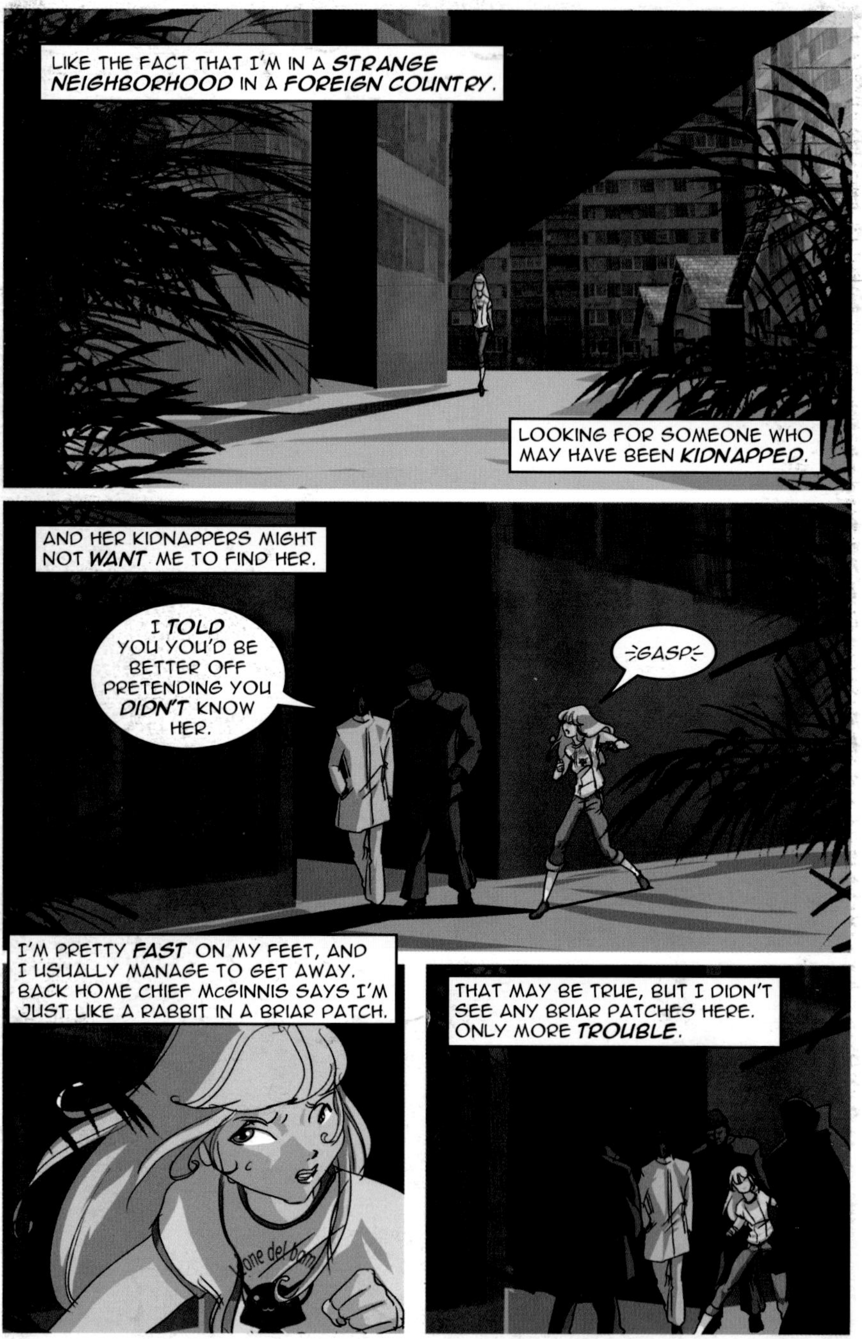
LIKE THE FACT THAT I'M IN A STRANGE NEIGHBORHOOD IN A FOREIGN COUNTRY.
LOOKING FOR SOMEONE WHO MAY HAVE BEEN KIDNAPPED.
AND HER KIDNAPPERS MIGHT NOT WANT ME TO FIND HER.
I TOLD YOU YOU'D BE BETTER OFF PRETENDING YOU DIDN'T KNOW HER.
GASP
I'M PRETTY FAST ON MY FEET, AND I USUALLY MANAGE TO GET AWAY. BACK HOME CHIEF McGINNIS SAYS I'M JUST LIKE A RABBIT IN A BRIAR PATCH.
THAT MAY BE TRUE, BUT I DIDN'T SEE ANY BRIAR PATCHES HERE. ONLY MORE TROUBLE.

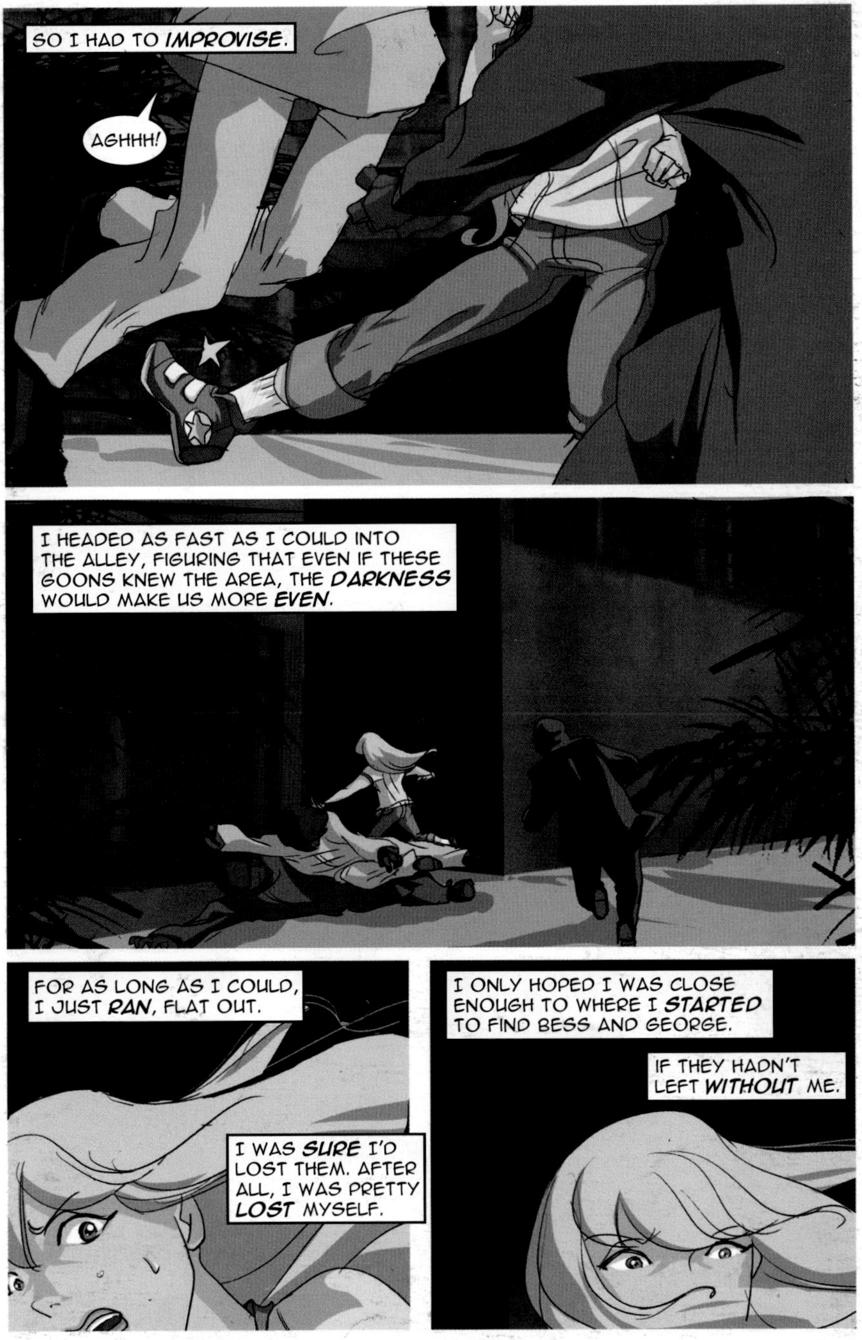
SO I HAD TO IMPROVISE.
AGHHH!
I HEADED AS FAST AS I COULD INTO THE ALLEY, FIGURING THAT EVEN IF THESE GOONS KNEW THE AREA, THE DARKNESS WOULD MAKE US MORE EVEN.
FOR AS LONG AS I COULD, I JUST RAN, FLAT OUT.
I WAS SURE I'D LOST THEM. AFTER ALL, I WAS PRETTY LOST MYSELF.
I ONLY HOPED I WAS CLOSE ENOUGH TO WHERE I STARTED TO FIND BESS AND GEORGE.
IF THEY HADN'T LEFT WITHOUT ME.

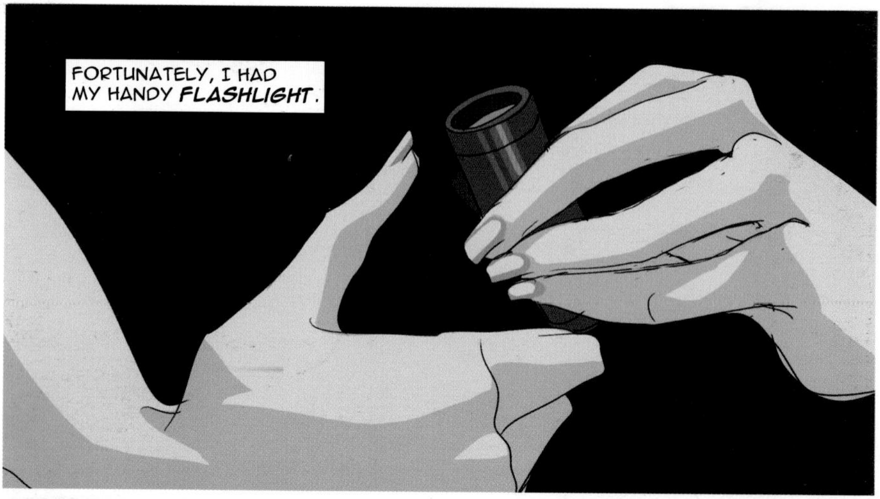
FORTUNATELY, I HAD MY HANDY FLASHLIGHT.
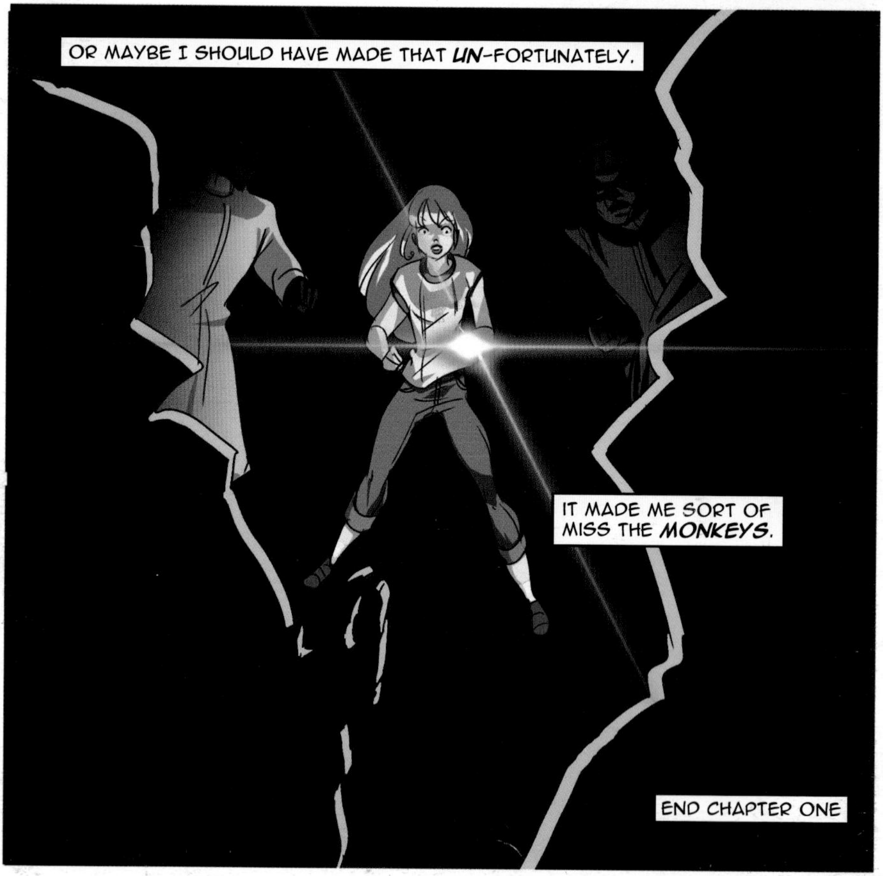
OR MAYBE I SHOULD HAVE MADE THAT UN-FORTUNATELY.
IT MADE ME SORT OF MISS THE MONKEYS.
END CHAPTER ONE

CHAPTER TWO: NANCY MAKES A SACRIFICE

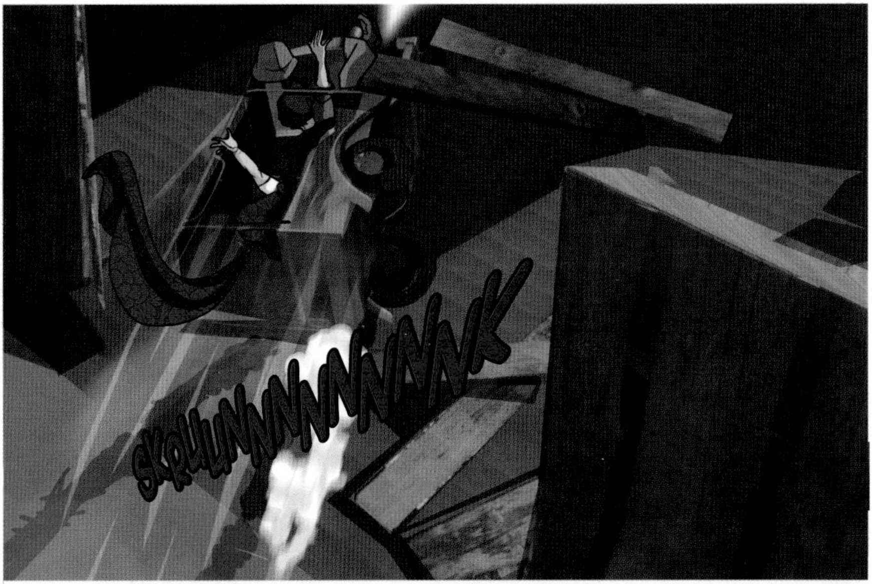
SKRUNNNNNNNNNK

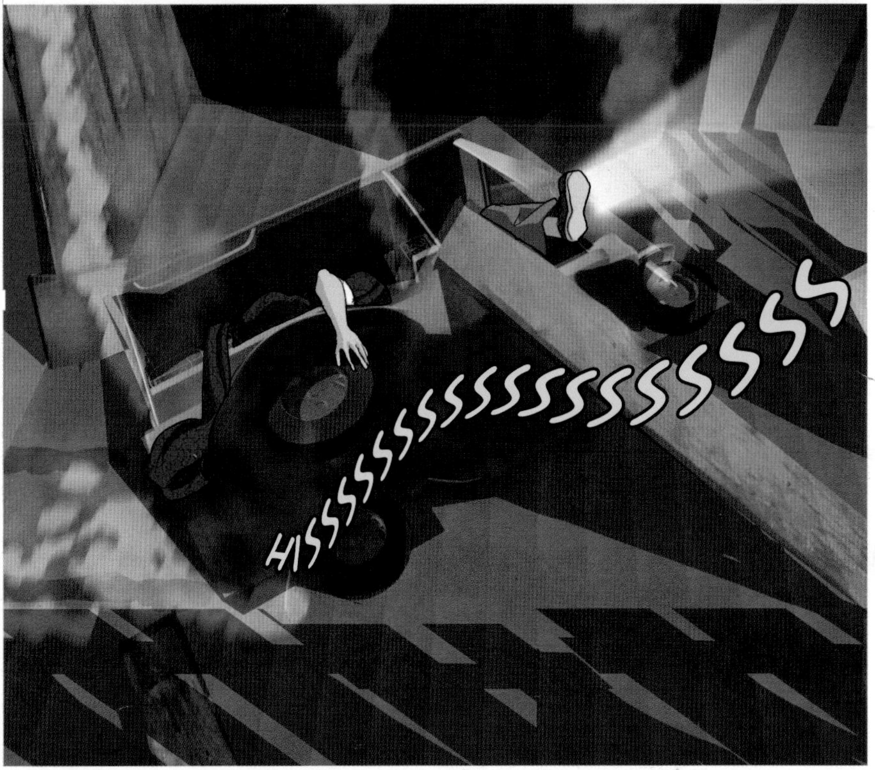
HISSSSSSSSSSSSSSSSSSS

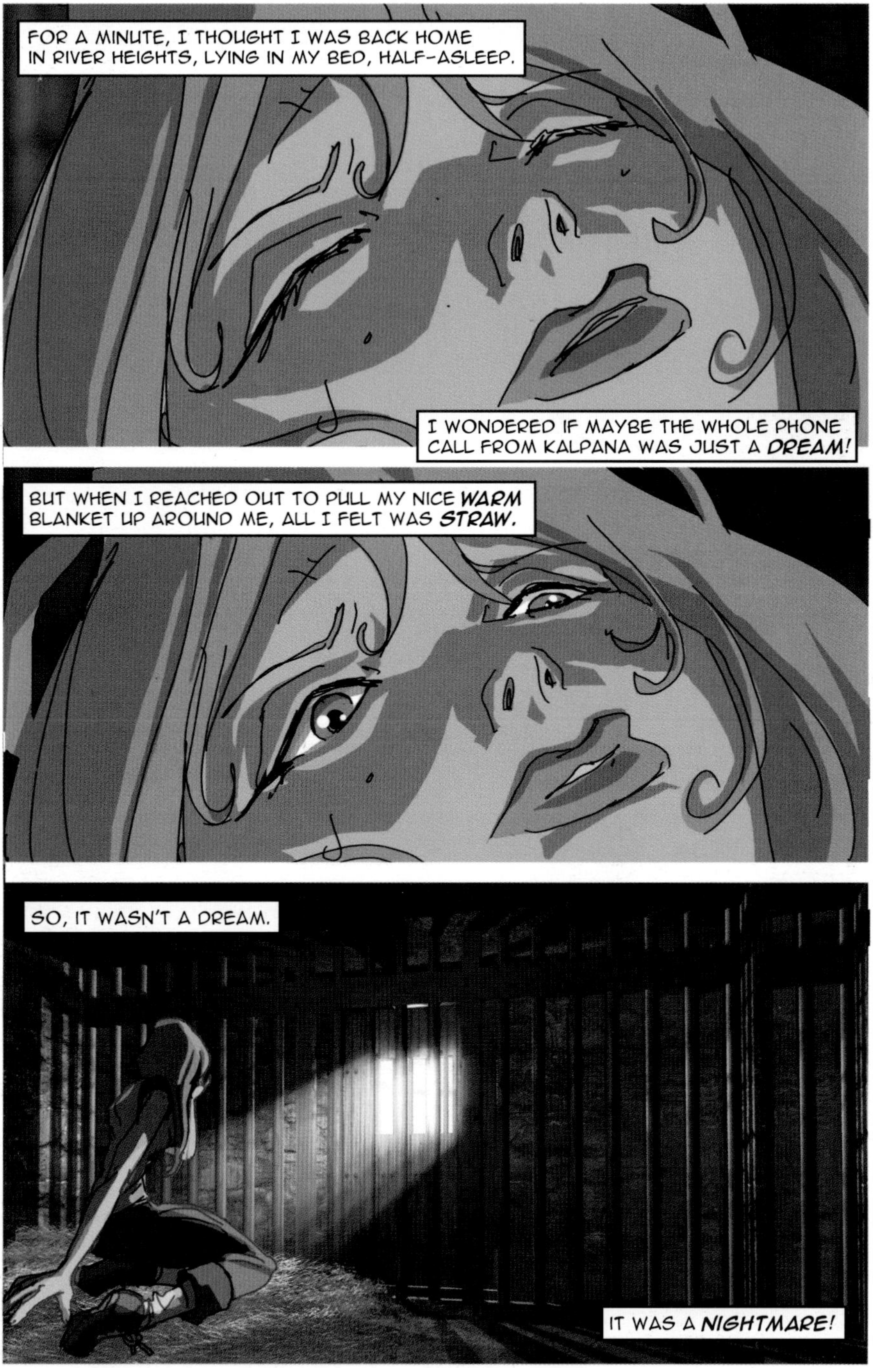
FOR A MINUTE, I THOUGHT I WAS BACK HOME IN RIVER HEIGHTS, LYING IN MY BED, HALF-ASLEEP.
I WONDERED IF MAYBE THE WHOLE PHONE CALL FROM KALPANA WAS JUST A *DREAM*!
BUT WHEN I REACHED OUT TO PULL MY NICE *WARM* BLANKET UP AROUND ME, ALL I FELT WAS *STRAW.*
SO, IT WASN'T A DREAM.
IT WAS A *NIGHTMARE*!

AWAKE? GOOD.

I AM SAHADEV, AND I WOULD LIKE *VERY MUCH* TO KNOW WHY YOU HAVE BEEN POKING AROUND MY *BUSINESS!*

IN A SITUATION LIKE THIS, I SAW NO *POINT* IN LYING!

I'M LOOKING FOR MY FRIEND, KALPANA! I MET HER ON THE PHONE, BACK IN THE UNITED STATES! SHE CALLED ME AND SAID SHE WAS IN DANGER!

I JUST WANT TO KNOW WHAT *HAPPENED* TO HER!

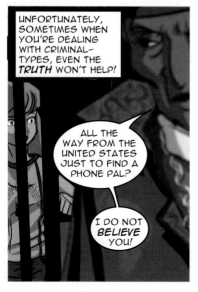

UNFORTUNATELY, SOMETIMES WHEN YOU'RE DEALING WITH CRIMINAL-TYPES, EVEN THE *TRUTH* WON'T HELP!

ALL THE WAY FROM THE UNITED STATES JUST TO FIND A PHONE PAL?

I DO NOT *BELIEVE* YOU!

SO I'LL ASK *AGAIN*, WHY ARE YOU HERE?

AND THIS TIME YOU'D *BETTER* TELL ME *EVERY-THING!*

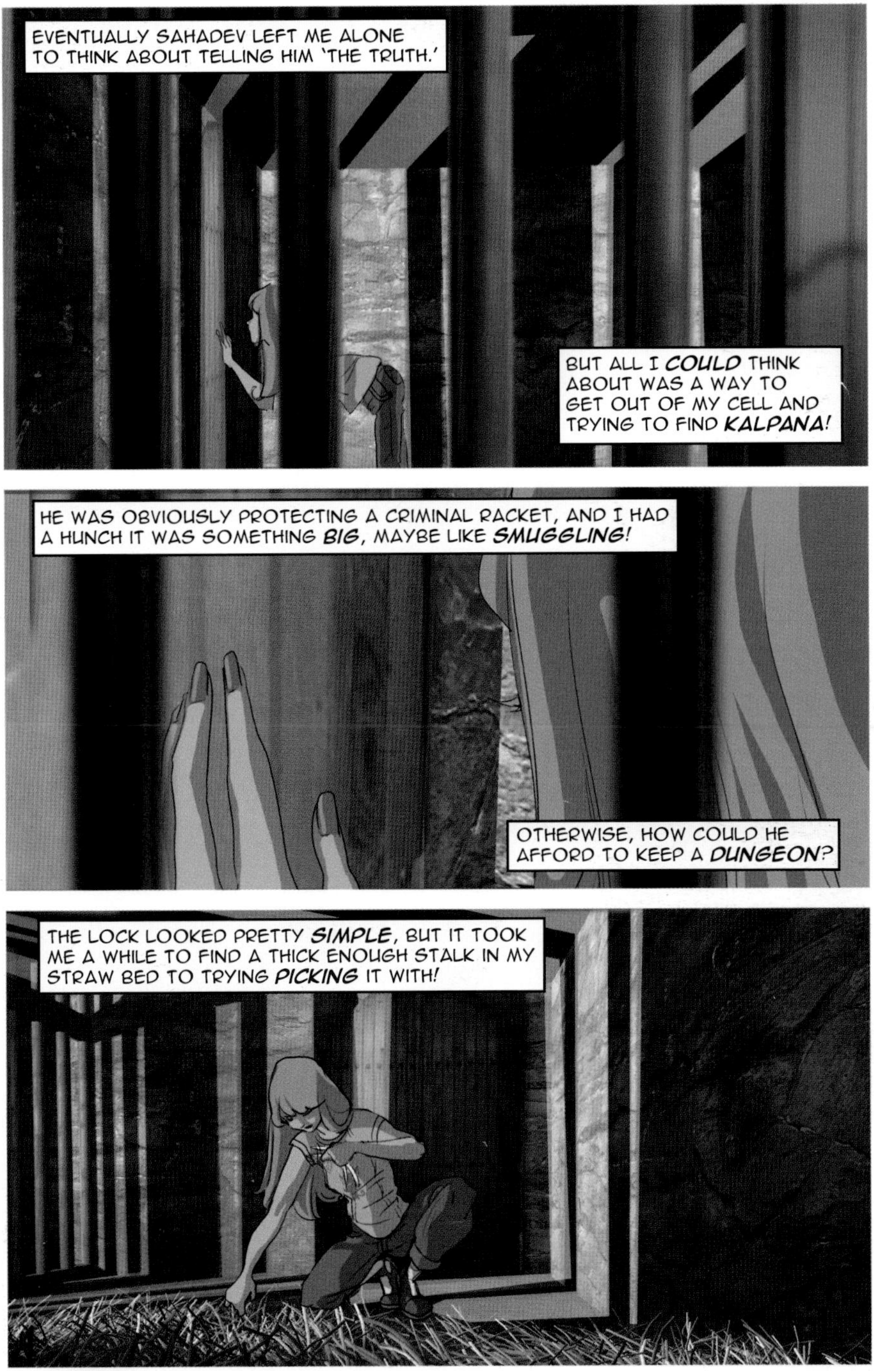
EVENTUALLY SAHADEV LEFT ME ALONE TO THINK ABOUT TELLING HIM 'THE TRUTH.'
BUT ALL I *COULD* THINK ABOUT WAS A WAY TO GET OUT OF MY CELL AND TRYING TO FIND *KALPANA*!
HE WAS OBVIOUSLY PROTECTING A CRIMINAL RACKET, AND I HAD A HUNCH IT WAS SOMETHING *BIG*, MAYBE LIKE *SMUGGLING*!
OTHERWISE, HOW COULD HE AFFORD TO KEEP A *DUNGEON*?
THE LOCK LOOKED PRETTY *SIMPLE*, BUT IT TOOK ME A WHILE TO FIND A THICK ENOUGH STALK IN MY STRAW BED TO TRYING *PICKING* IT WITH!

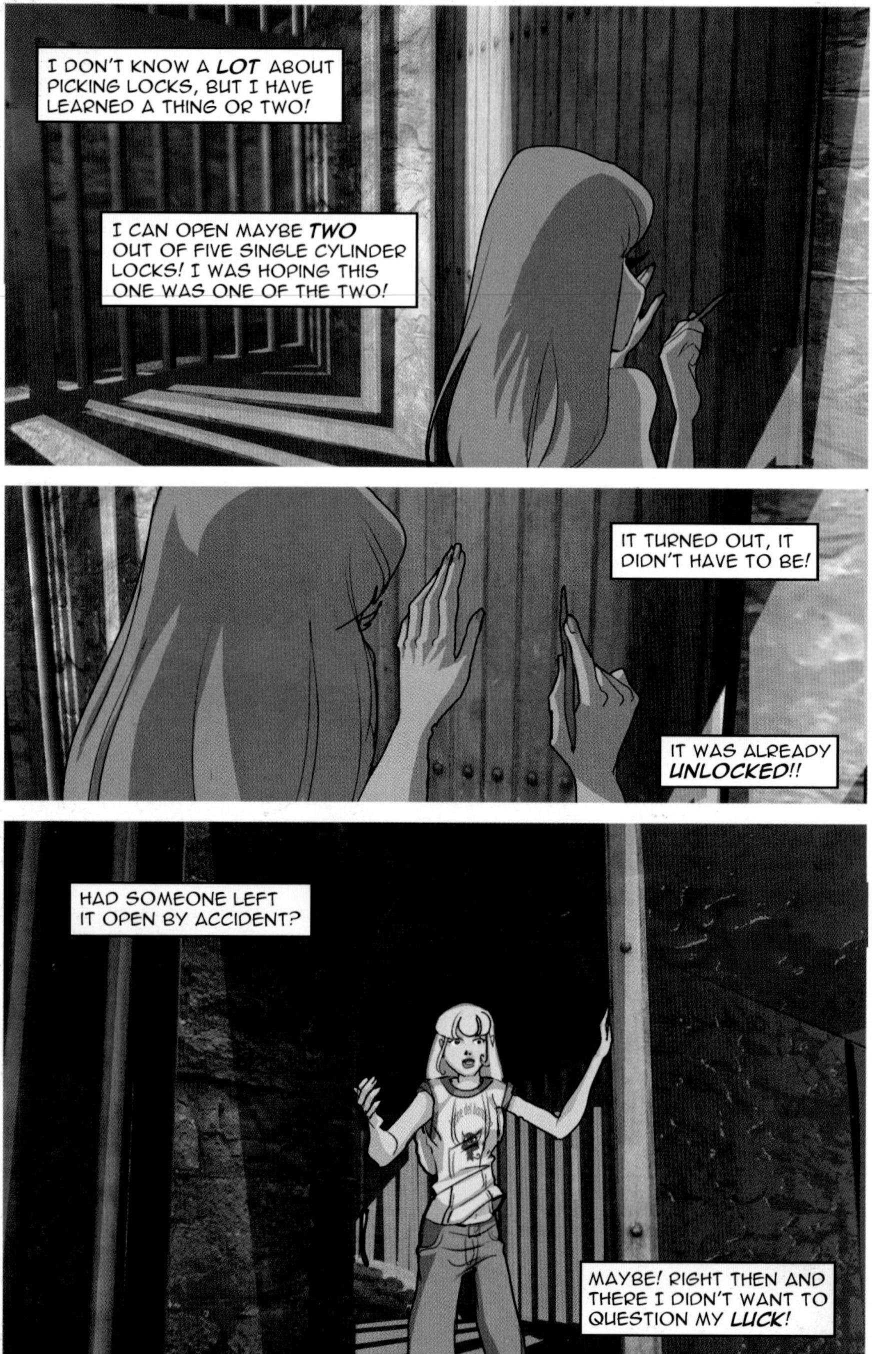
I DON'T KNOW A LOT ABOUT PICKING LOCKS, BUT I HAVE LEARNED A THING OR TWO!
I CAN OPEN MAYBE TWO OUT OF FIVE SINGLE CYLINDER LOCKS! I WAS HOPING THIS ONE WAS ONE OF THE TWO!
IT TURNED OUT, IT DIDN'T HAVE TO BE!
IT WAS ALREADY UNLOCKED!!
HAD SOMEONE LEFT IT OPEN BY ACCIDENT?
MAYBE! RIGHT THEN AND THERE I DIDN'T WANT TO QUESTION MY LUCK!

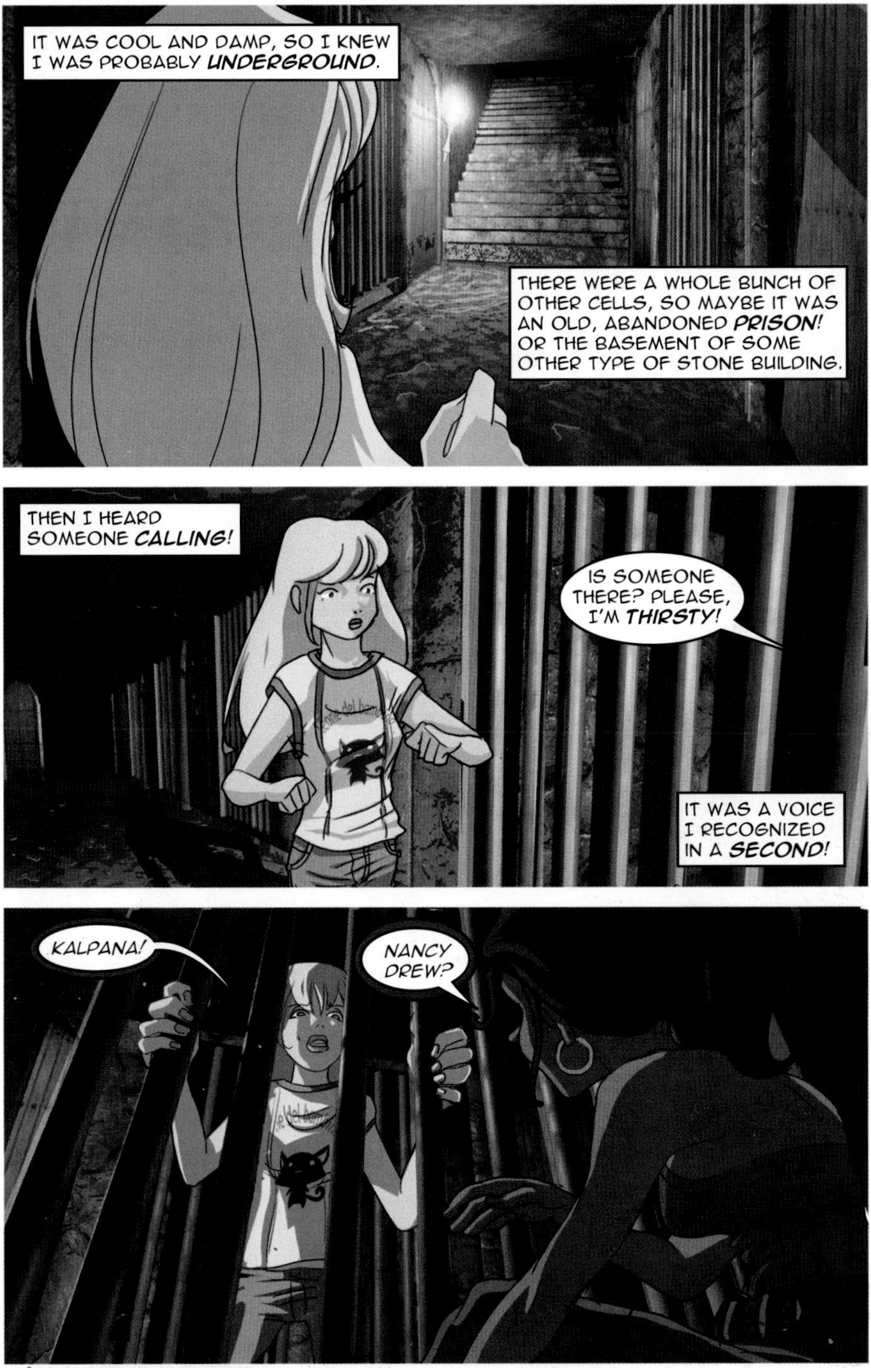
IT WAS COOL AND DAMP, SO I KNEW I WAS PROBABLY UNDERGROUND.
THERE WERE A WHOLE BUNCH OF OTHER CELLS, SO MAYBE IT WAS AN OLD, ABANDONED PRISON! OR THE BASEMENT OF SOME OTHER TYPE OF STONE BUILDING.
THEN I HEARD SOMEONE CALLING!
IS SOMEONE THERE? PLEASE, I'M THIRSTY!
IT WAS A VOICE I RECOGNIZED IN A SECOND!
KALPANA!
NANCY DREW?

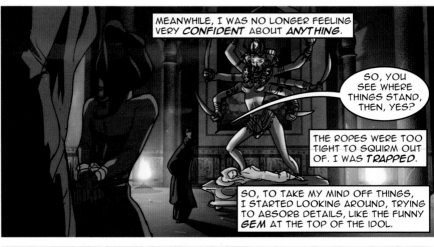

MEANWHILE, I WAS NO LONGER FEELING VERY **CONFIDENT** ABOUT **ANYTHING.**

SO, YOU SEE WHERE THINGS STAND, THEN, YES?

THE ROPES WERE TOO TIGHT TO SQUIRM OUT OF. I WAS **TRAPPED.**

SO, TO TAKE MY MIND OFF THINGS, I STARTED LOOKING AROUND, TRYING TO ABSORB DETAILS, LIKE THE FUNNY **GEM** AT THE TOP OF THE IDOL.

THIS IS **CRAZY!** NO ONE SACRIFICES TO KALI ANYMORE!

AND THE **FEAR** MIXED WITH **BRAVERY** IN KALPANA'S VOICE.

OH, YOU'RE QUITE **WRONG** ABOUT THAT.

MANY USE ANIMALS, OR **SYMBOLS** TODAY, BUT THERE ARE STILL **PURISTS** AMONG US!

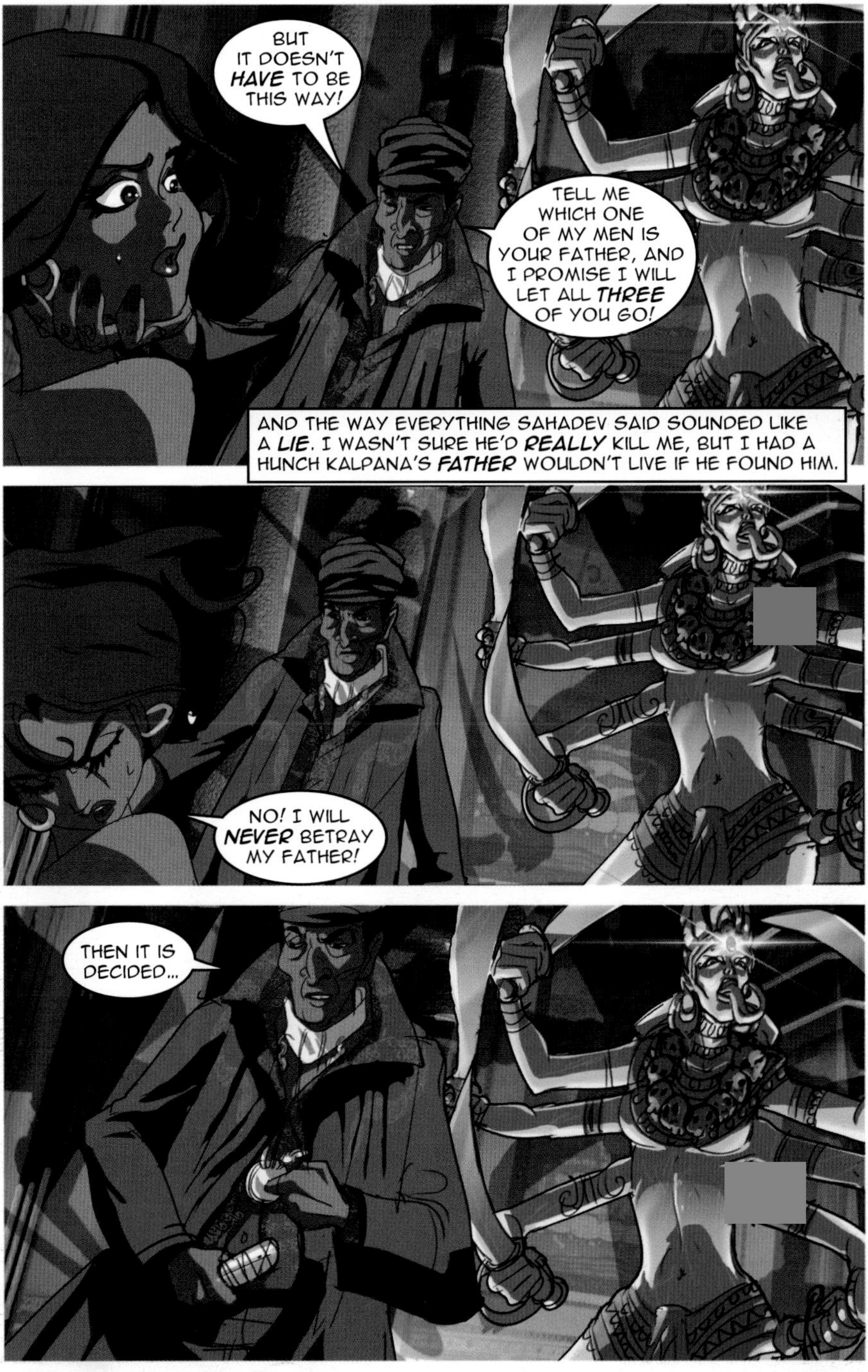
BUT IT DOESN'T *HAVE* TO BE THIS WAY!
TELL ME WHICH ONE OF MY MEN IS YOUR FATHER, AND I PROMISE I WILL LET ALL *THREE* OF YOU GO!
AND THE WAY EVERYTHING SAHADEV SAID SOUNDED LIKE A *LIE*. I WASN'T SURE HE'D *REALLY* KILL ME, BUT I HAD A HUNCH KALPANA'S *FATHER* WOULDN'T LIVE IF HE FOUND HIM.
NO! I WILL *NEVER* BETRAY MY FATHER!
THEN IT IS DECIDED...

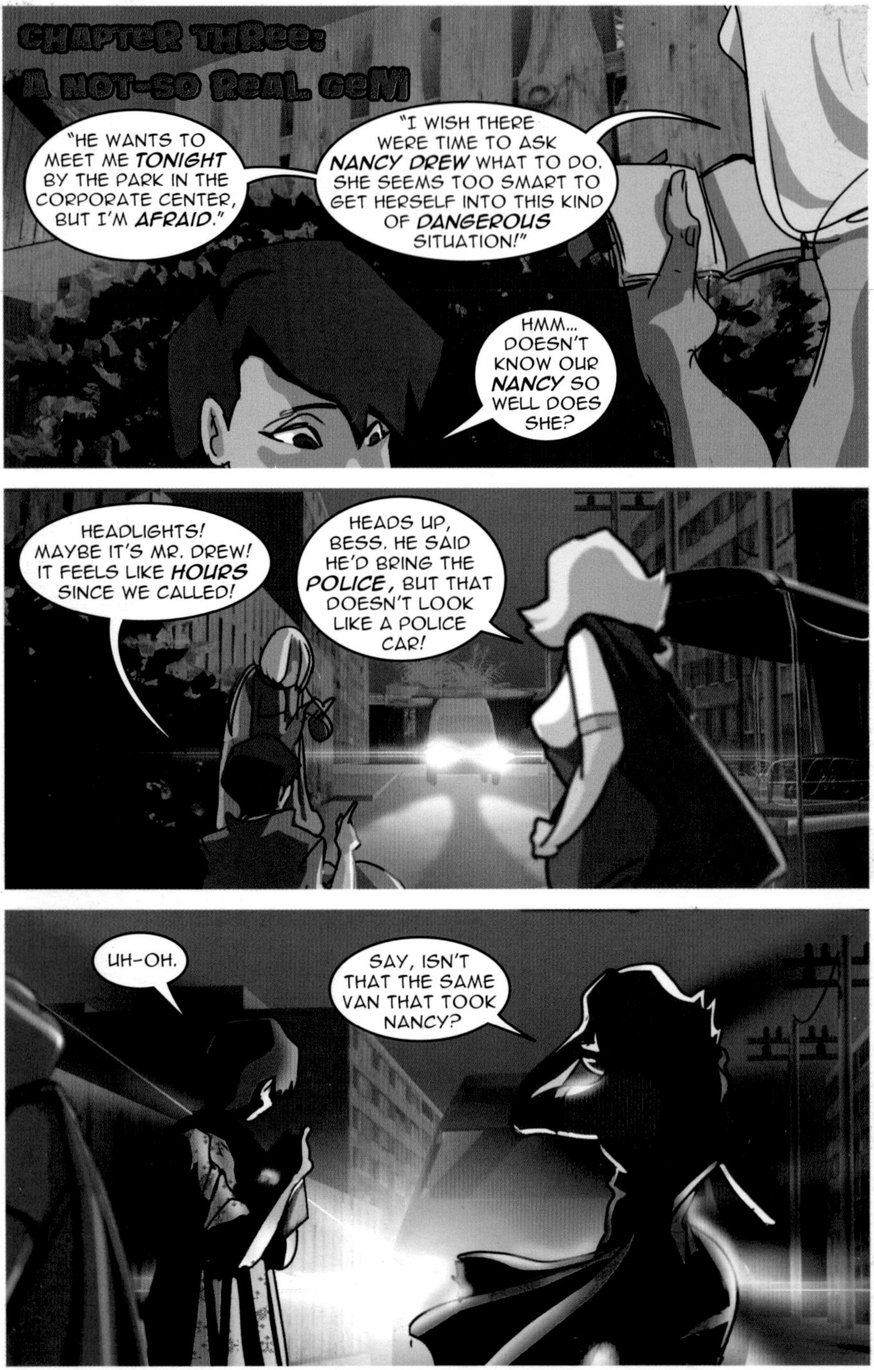
CHAPTER THREE:
A NOT-SO REAL GEM
"HE WANTS TO MEET ME TONIGHT BY THE PARK IN THE CORPORATE CENTER, BUT I'M AFRAID."
"I WISH THERE WERE TIME TO ASK NANCY DREW WHAT TO DO. SHE SEEMS TOO SMART TO GET HERSELF INTO THIS KIND OF DANGEROUS SITUATION!"
HMM... DOESN'T KNOW OUR NANCY SO WELL DOES SHE?
HEADLIGHTS! MAYBE IT'S MR. DREW! IT FEELS LIKE HOURS SINCE WE CALLED!
HEADS UP, BESS. HE SAID HE'D BRING THE POLICE, BUT THAT DOESN'T LOOK LIKE A POLICE CAR!
UH-OH.
SAY, ISN'T THAT THE SAME VAN THAT TOOK NANCY?

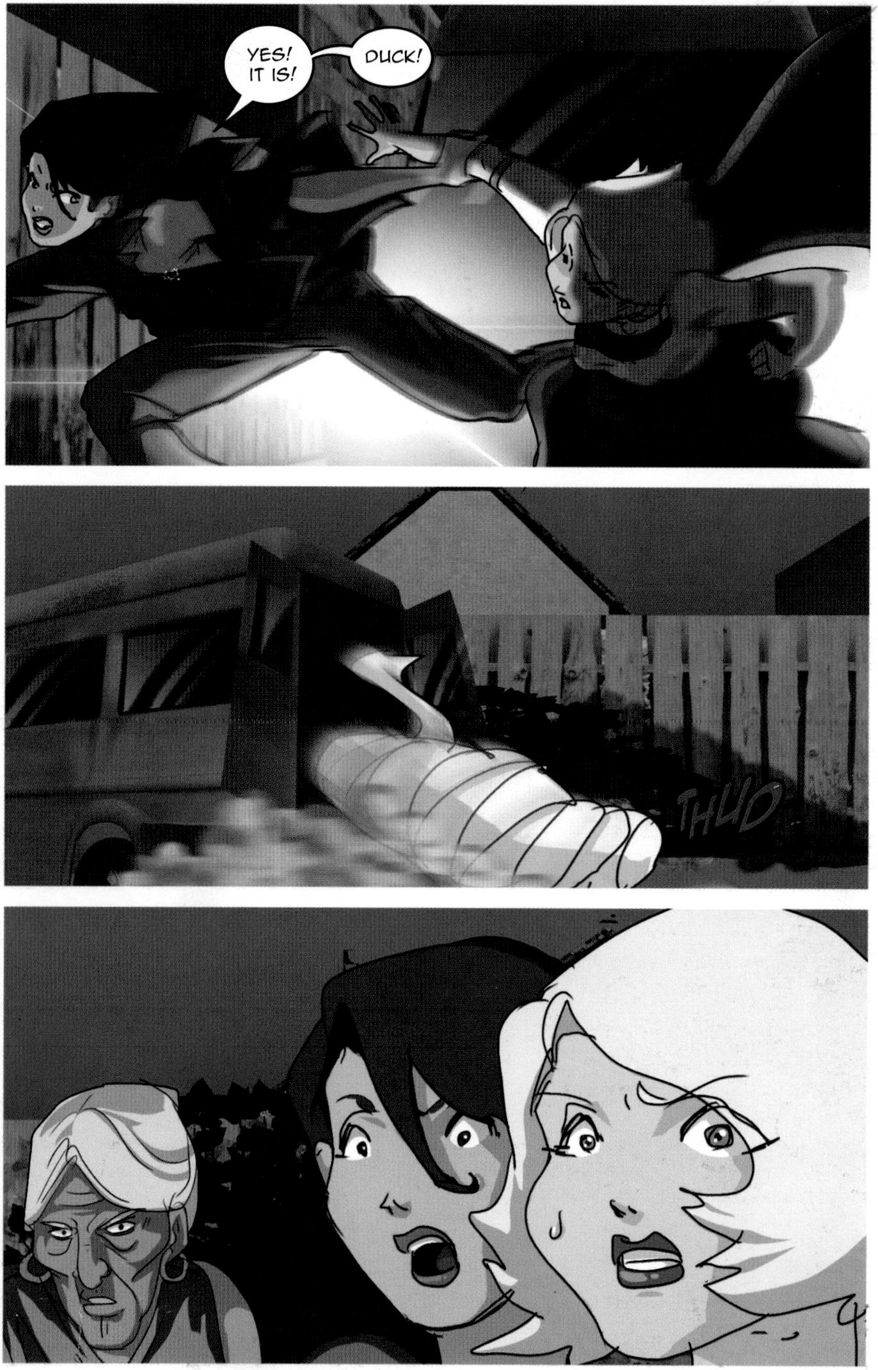
YES! IT IS!
DUCK!
THUD

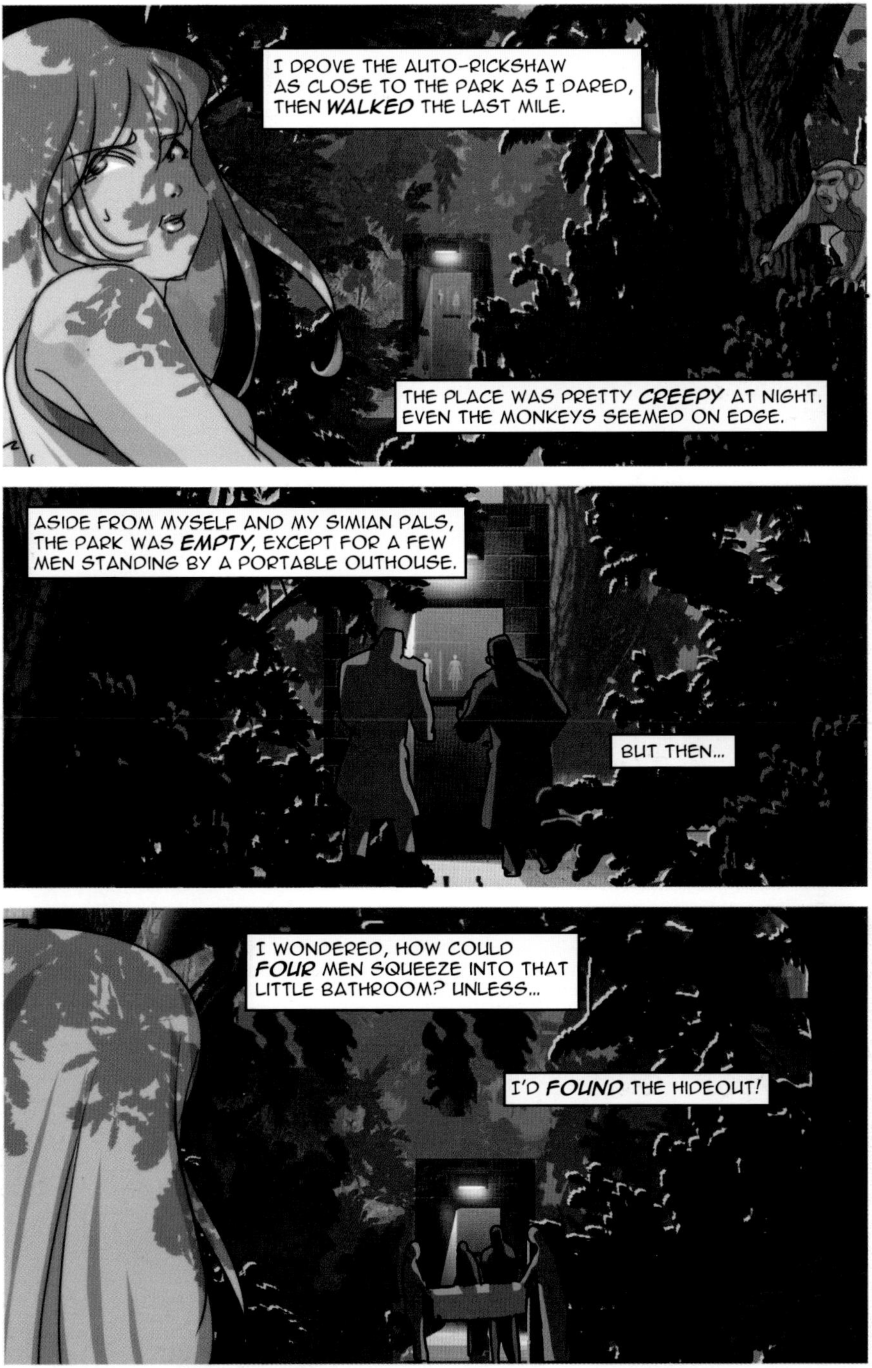
I DROVE THE AUTO-RICKSHAW AS CLOSE TO THE PARK AS I DARED, THEN WALKED THE LAST MILE.
THE PLACE WAS PRETTY CREEPY AT NIGHT. EVEN THE MONKEYS SEEMED ON EDGE.
ASIDE FROM MYSELF AND MY SIMIAN PALS, THE PARK WAS EMPTY, EXCEPT FOR A FEW MEN STANDING BY A PORTABLE OUTHOUSE.
BUT THEN...
I WONDERED, HOW COULD FOUR MEN SQUEEZE INTO THAT LITTLE BATHROOM? UNLESS...
I'D FOUND THE HIDEOUT!

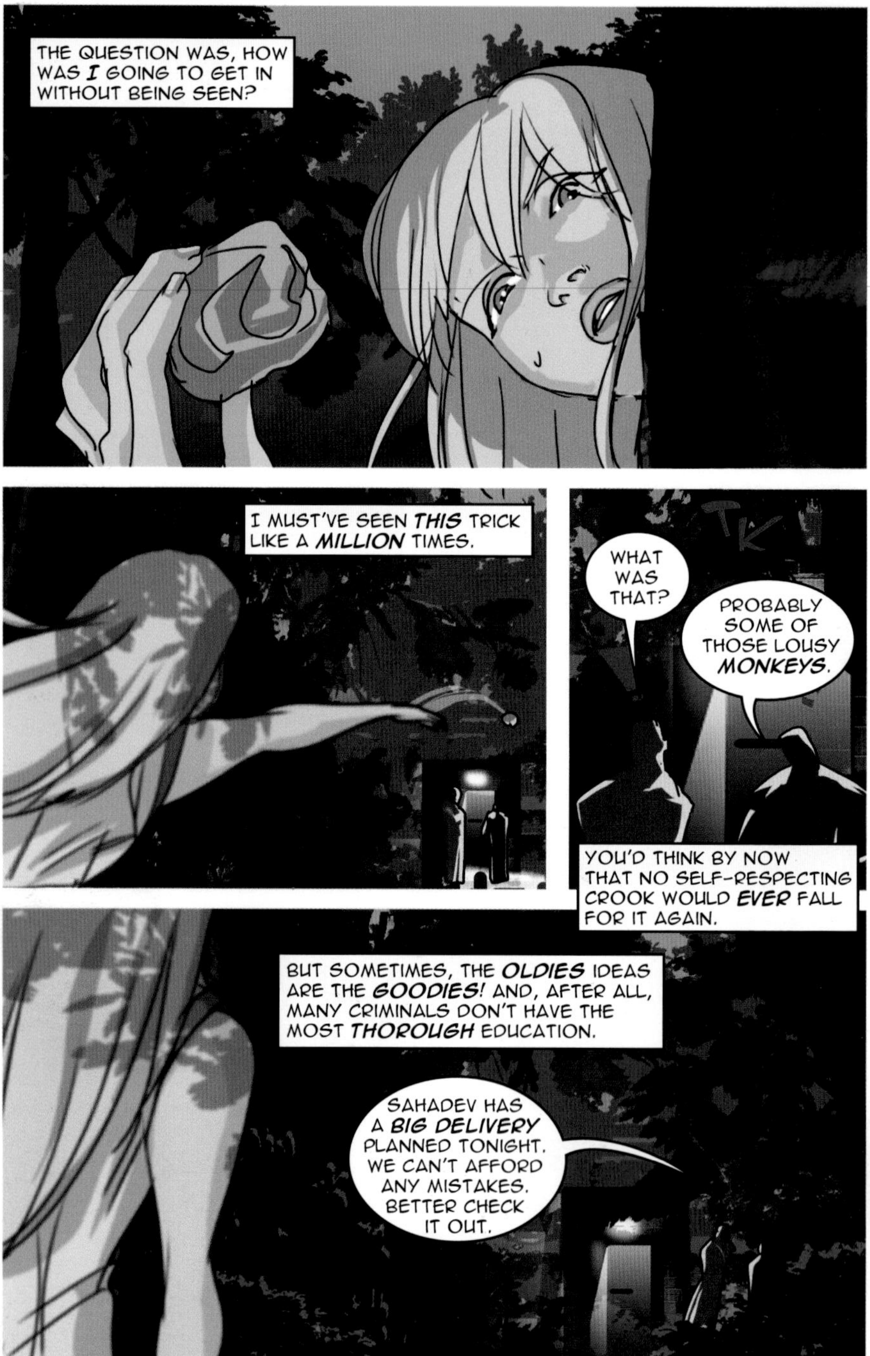
THE QUESTION WAS, HOW WAS I GOING TO GET IN WITHOUT BEING SEEN?
I MUST'VE SEEN THIS TRICK LIKE A MILLION TIMES.
TK!
WHAT WAS THAT?
PROBABLY SOME OF THOSE LOUSY MONKEYS.
YOU'D THINK BY NOW THAT NO SELF-RESPECTING CROOK WOULD EVER FALL FOR IT AGAIN.
BUT SOMETIMES, THE OLDIES IDEAS ARE THE GOODIES! AND, AFTER ALL, MANY CRIMINALS DON'T HAVE THE MOST THOROUGH EDUCATION.
SAHADEV HAS A BIG DELIVERY PLANNED TONIGHT. WE CAN'T AFFORD ANY MISTAKES. BETTER CHECK IT OUT.

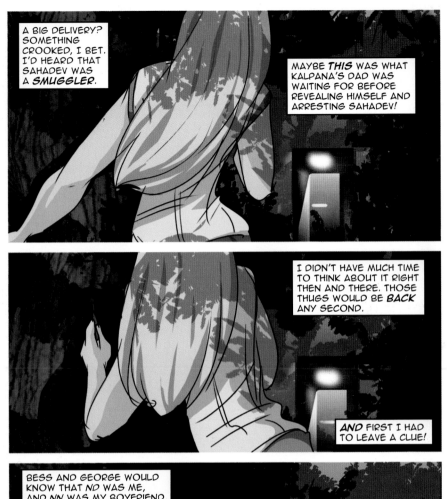

A BIG DELIVERY? SOMETHING CROOKED, I BET. I'D HEARD THAT SAHADEV WAS A *SMUGGLER*.

MAYBE *THIS* WAS WHAT KALPANA'S DAD WAS WAITING FOR BEFORE REVEALING HIMSELF AND ARRESTING SAHADEV!

I DIDN'T HAVE MUCH TIME TO THINK ABOUT IT RIGHT THEN AND THERE. THOSE THUGS WOULD BE *BACK* ANY SECOND.

AND FIRST I HAD TO LEAVE A CLUE!

BESS AND GEORGE WOULD KNOW THAT *ND* WAS ME, AND *NN* WAS MY BOYFRIEND, *NED NICKERSON!*

I ONLY HOPED THEY'D *ALSO* REALIZE CUPID'S ARROW WAS POINTED RIGHT AT THE DOOR TO THE *HIDEOUT!*

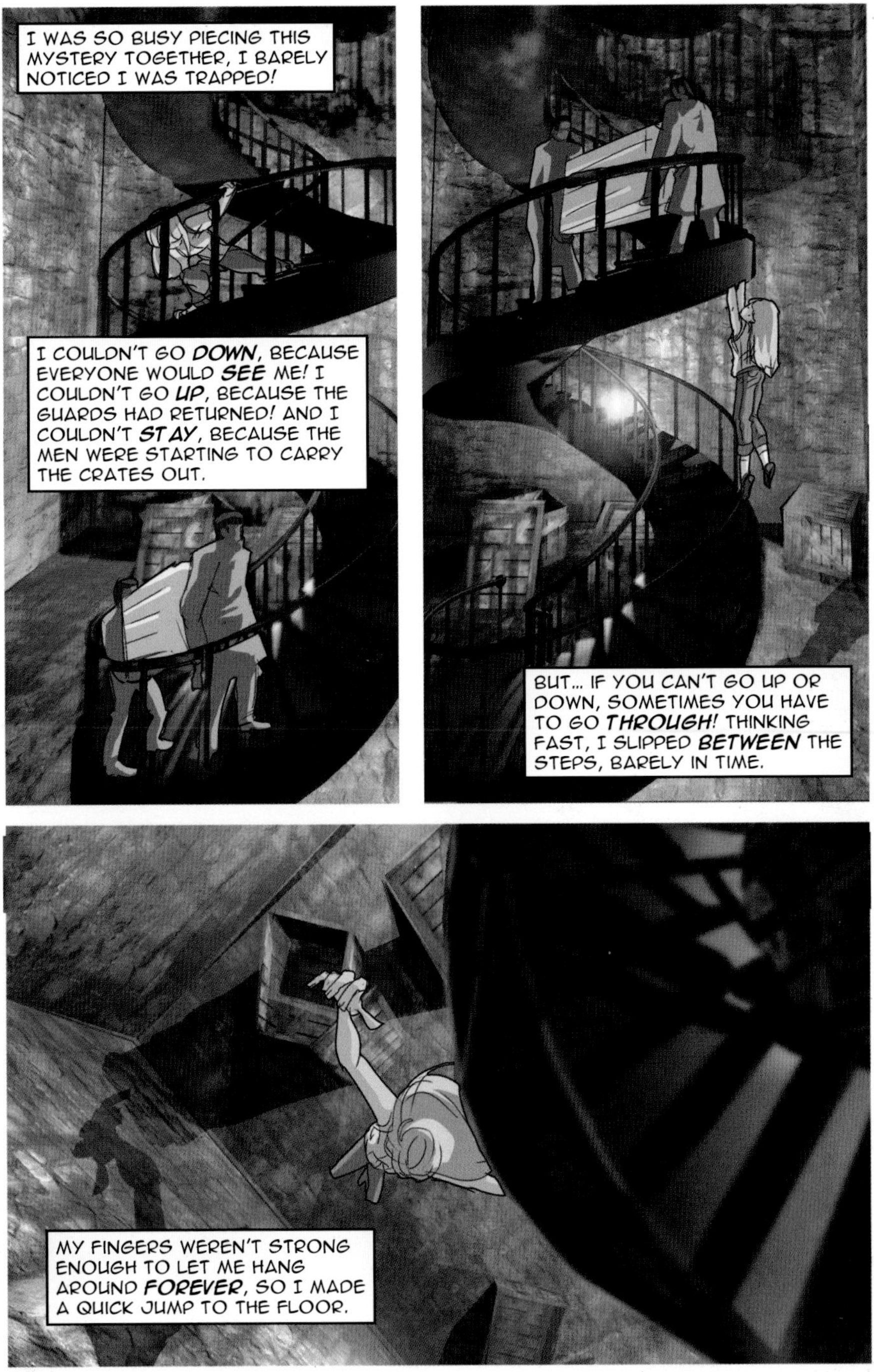

I WAS SO BUSY PIECING THIS MYSTERY TOGETHER, I BARELY NOTICED I WAS TRAPPED!
I COULDN'T GO *DOWN*, BECAUSE EVERYONE WOULD *SEE* ME! I COULDN'T GO *UP*, BECAUSE THE GUARDS HAD RETURNED! AND I COULDN'T *STAY*, BECAUSE THE MEN WERE STARTING TO CARRY THE CRATES OUT.
BUT... IF YOU CAN'T GO UP OR DOWN, SOMETIMES YOU HAVE TO GO *THROUGH*! THINKING FAST, I SLIPPED *BETWEEN* THE STEPS, BARELY IN TIME.
MY FINGERS WEREN'T STRONG ENOUGH TO LET ME HANG AROUND *FOREVER*, SO I MADE A QUICK JUMP TO THE FLOOR.

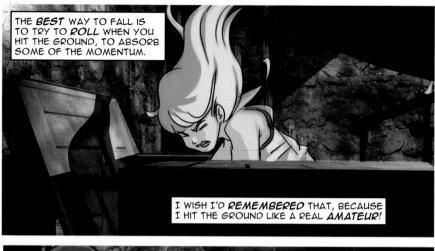

THE **BEST** WAY TO FALL IS TO TRY TO **ROLL** WHEN YOU HIT THE GROUND, TO ABSORB SOME OF THE MOMENTUM.

I WISH I'D **REMEMBERED** THAT, BECAUSE I HIT THE GROUND LIKE A REAL **AMATEUR!**

THIS WAS NO TIME TO FEEL SORRY FOR MYSELF THOUGH. THERE WAS **KALPANA!**

EVERYONE'S BUSY, BUT THEY WON'T BE **FOREVER**, SO WE'VE GOT JUST A FEW **SECONDS** TO GET YOU OUT OF HERE!

NANCY!

SHHH!

GREAT! BUT HOW? WE'RE TOTALLY **SURROUND-ED!**

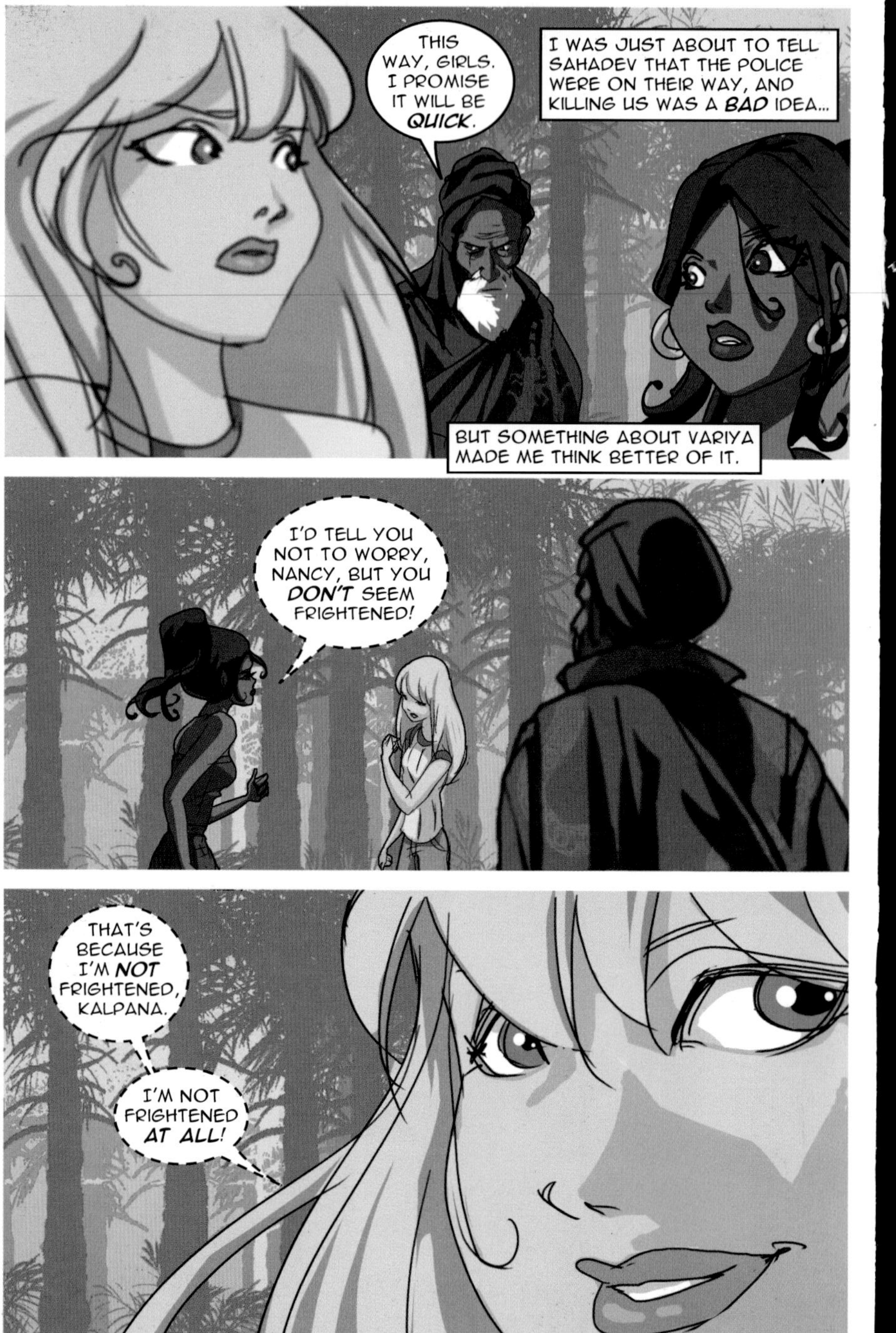
THIS WAY, GIRLS. I PROMISE IT WILL BE QUICK.
I WAS JUST ABOUT TO TELL SAHADEV THAT THE POLICE WERE ON THEIR WAY, AND KILLING US WAS A BAD IDEA...
BUT SOMETHING ABOUT VARIYA MADE ME THINK BETTER OF IT.
I'D TELL YOU NOT TO WORRY, NANCY, BUT YOU DON'T SEEM FRIGHTENED!
THAT'S BECAUSE I'M NOT FRIGHTENED, KALPANA.
I'M NOT FRIGHTENED AT ALL!

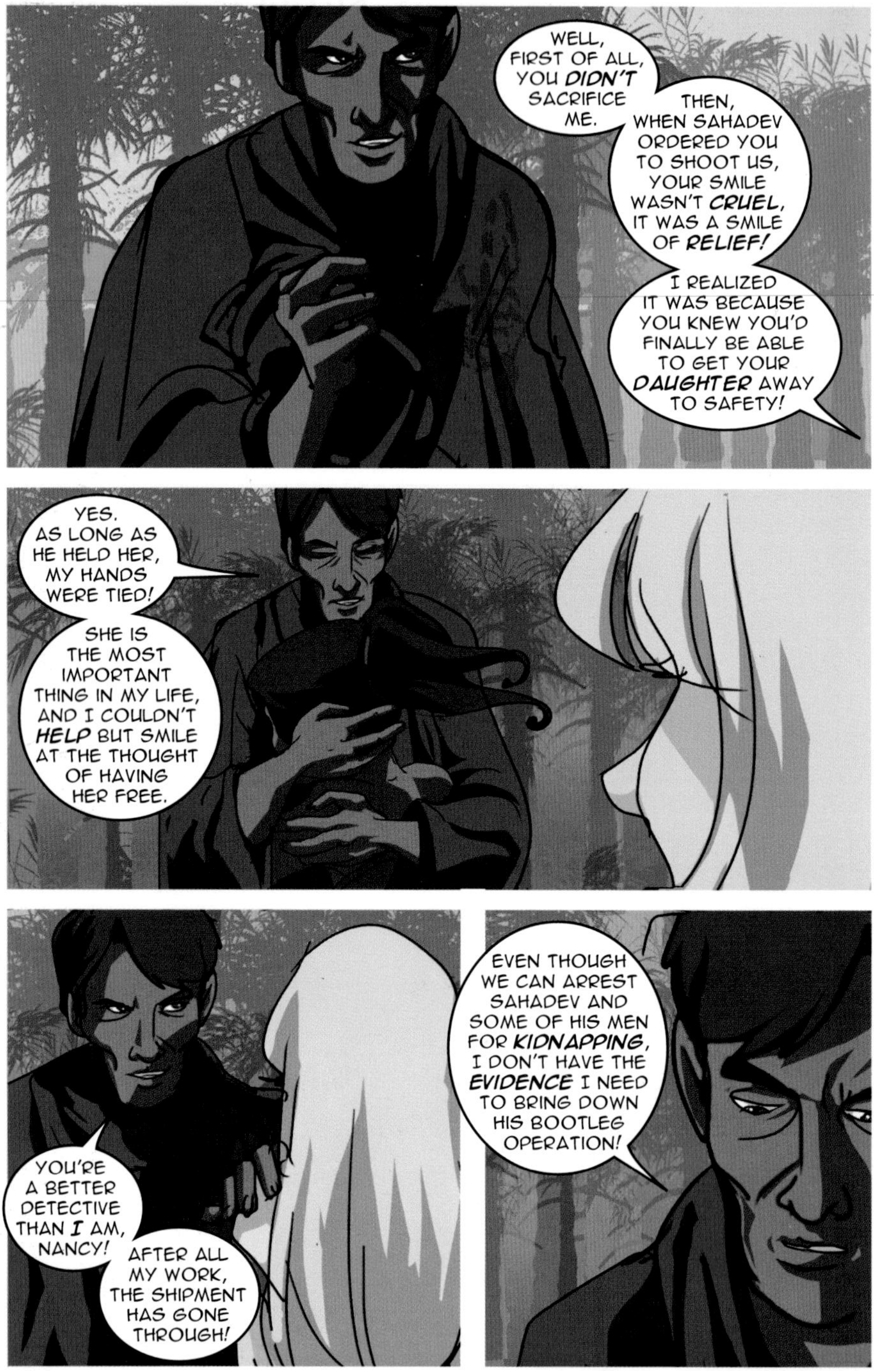
WELL, FIRST OF ALL, YOU DIDN'T SACRIFICE ME.
THEN, WHEN SAHADEV ORDERED YOU TO SHOOT US, YOUR SMILE WASN'T CRUEL, IT WAS A SMILE OF RELIEF!
I REALIZED IT WAS BECAUSE YOU KNEW YOU'D FINALLY BE ABLE TO GET YOUR DAUGHTER AWAY TO SAFETY!
YES. AS LONG AS HE HELD HER, MY HANDS WERE TIED!
SHE IS THE MOST IMPORTANT THING IN MY LIFE, AND I COULDN'T HELP BUT SMILE AT THE THOUGHT OF HAVING HER FREE.
YOU'RE A BETTER DETECTIVE THAN I AM, NANCY!
AFTER ALL MY WORK, THE SHIPMENT HAS GONE THROUGH!
EVEN THOUGH WE CAN ARREST SAHADEV AND SOME OF HIS MEN FOR KIDNAPPING, I DON'T HAVE THE EVIDENCE I NEED TO BRING DOWN HIS BOOTLEG OPERATION!

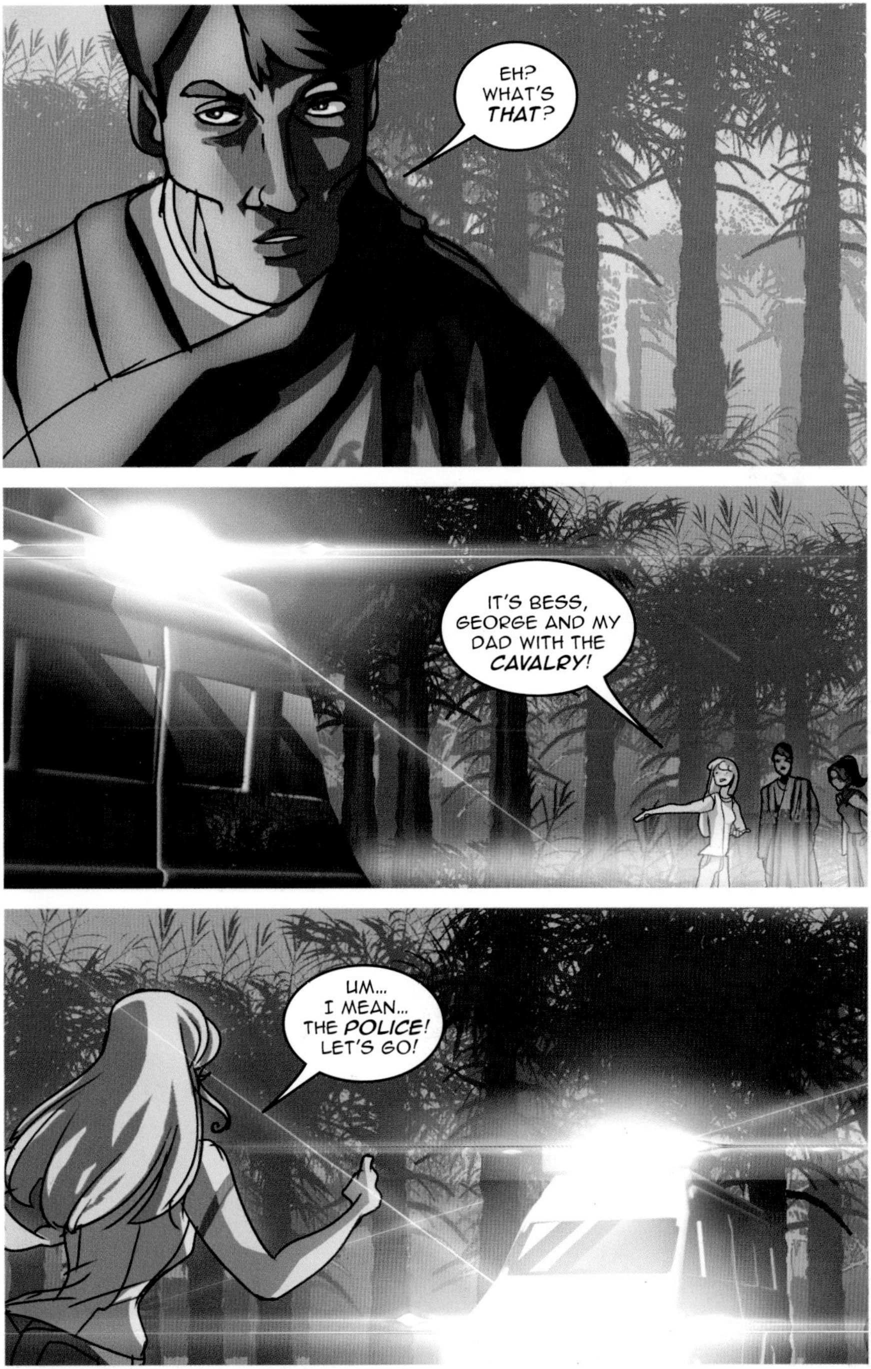
EH? WHAT'S *THAT*?
IT'S BESS, GEORGE AND MY DAD WITH THE *CAVALRY*!
UM... I MEAN... THE *POLICE*! LET'S GO!

KALPANA'S DAD DIDN'T HAVE ENOUGH EVIDENCE TO BRING DOWN THE OPERATION, BUT I HAD A HUNCH WHERE I MIGHT FIND *SOME!*

THE *GEM* ON THE STATUE OF KALI LOOKED A LITTLE FUNNY TO ME LAST TIME I LOOKED TO PAY IT.

AND THAT'S BECAUSE IT WAS *FAKE!*

IT JUST GOES TO SHOW YOU HOW IMPORTANT IT IS TO PAY *ATTENTION*, EVEN IF YOU ARE ABOUT TO BE SACRIFICED TO A HINDU GODDESS!

I ONLY HOPED WHATEVER ALL THIS STUFF WAS THAT IT WOULD *HELP!*

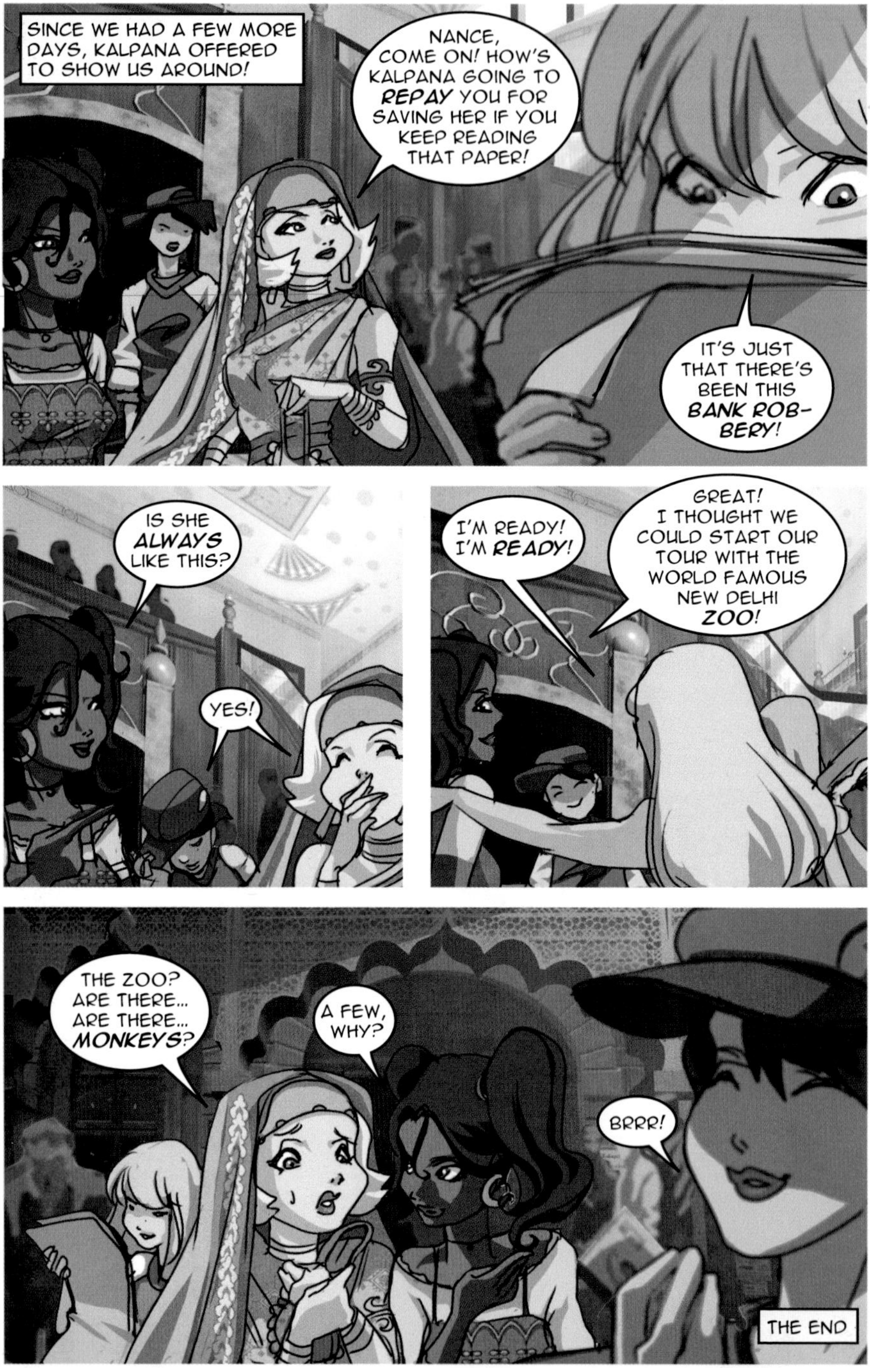
SINCE WE HAD A FEW MORE DAYS, KALPANA OFFERED TO SHOW US AROUND!
NANCE, COME ON! HOW'S KALPANA GOING TO REPAY YOU FOR SAVING HER IF YOU KEEP READING THAT PAPER!
IT'S JUST THAT THERE'S BEEN THIS BANK ROBBERY!
IS SHE ALWAYS LIKE THIS?
YES!
I'M READY! I'M READY!
GREAT! I THOUGHT WE COULD START OUR TOUR WITH THE WORLD FAMOUS NEW DELHI ZOO!
THE ZOO? ARE THERE... ARE THERE... MONKEYS?
A FEW, WHY?
BRRR!
THE END

Don't miss NANCY DREW Graphic Novel # 5 – "The Fake Heir".

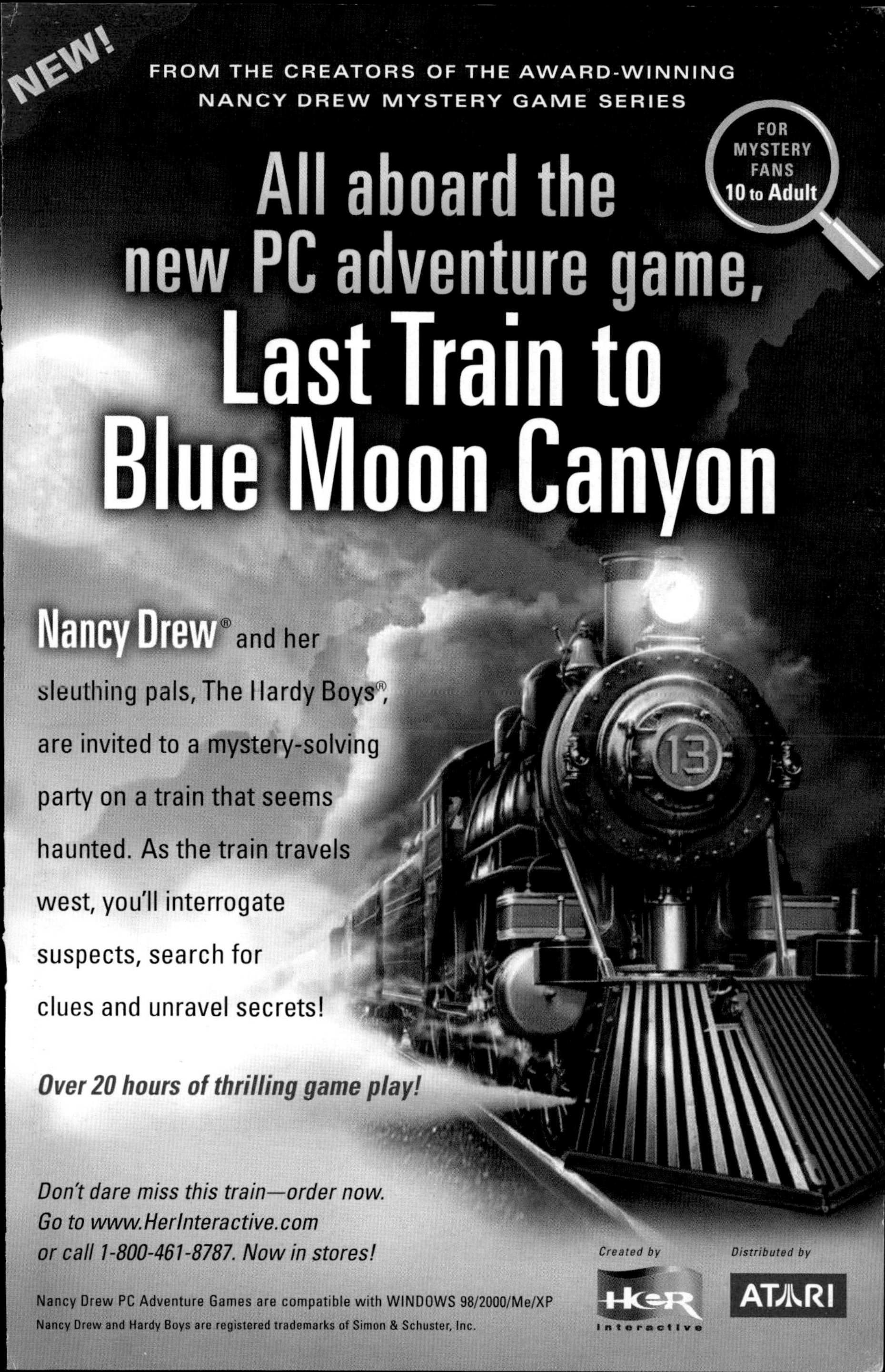
NEW!
FROM THE CREATORS OF THE AWARD-WINNING
NANCY DREW MYSTERY GAME SERIES
FOR MYSTERY FANS 10 to Adult
All aboard the
new PC adventure game,
Last Train to
Blue Moon Canyon
Nancy Drew® and her
sleuthing pals, The Hardy Boys®,
are invited to a mystery-solving
party on a train that seems
haunted. As the train travels
west, you'll interrogate
suspects, search for
clues and unravel secrets!
Over 20 hours of thrilling game play!
13
Don't dare miss this train—order now.
Go to www.HerInteractive.com
or call 1-800-461-8787. Now in stores!
Created by
HER Interactive
Distributed by
ATARI
Nancy Drew PC Adventure Games are compatible with WINDOWS 98/2000/Me/XP
Nancy Drew and Hardy Boys are registered trademarks of Simon & Schuster, Inc.

THE HARDY BOYS

A NEW GRAPHIC NOVEL EVERY 3 MONTHS!

#1 "The Ocean of Osyria"
ISBN 1-59707-001-7

#2 "Identity Theft"
ISBN 1-59707-003-3

#3 "Mad House"
ISBN 1-59707-010-6

NEW! **#4 "Malled"**
Frank, Joe, and seven others are mysteriously locked in the mall - with a murderer on the loose!
ISBN 1-59707-014-9

Each: 5x7 1/2, 96pp., full color paperback: $7.95

Also available in hardcover!
$12.95 each.
Vol. 1: ISBN 1-59707-005-X
Vol. 2: ISBN 1-59707-007-6
Vol. 3: ISBN 1-59707-011-4
Vol. 4: ISBN 1-59707-015-7

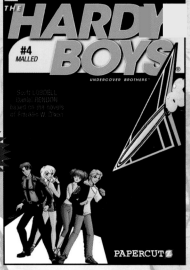

ZORRO®

#1 "Scars!"
ISBN 1-59707-016-5
NEW! **#2 "Drownings!"**
Zorro and Eulalia Bandini plunge into an icy chasm that threatens to become their glacial coffin!
And somehow, between being buried alive and drowning, Eulalia attempts to unmask Zorro!
ISBN 1-59707-018-1

Each: 5x7 1/2, 96pp., full color paperback: $7.95

Also available in hardcover!
$12.95 each.
Vol. 1: ISBN 1-59707-017-3
Vol. 2: ISBN 1-59707-019-X

PAPERCUTZ™

At your store or order at Papercutz,
555 8th Ave., Ste. 1202, New York, NY
10018, 1-800-886-1223 (M-F 9-6 EST)

MC, VISA, AMEX accepted, add $3 P&H for 1st item, $1 each additional.
Distributed by Holtzbrinck

www.papercutz.com

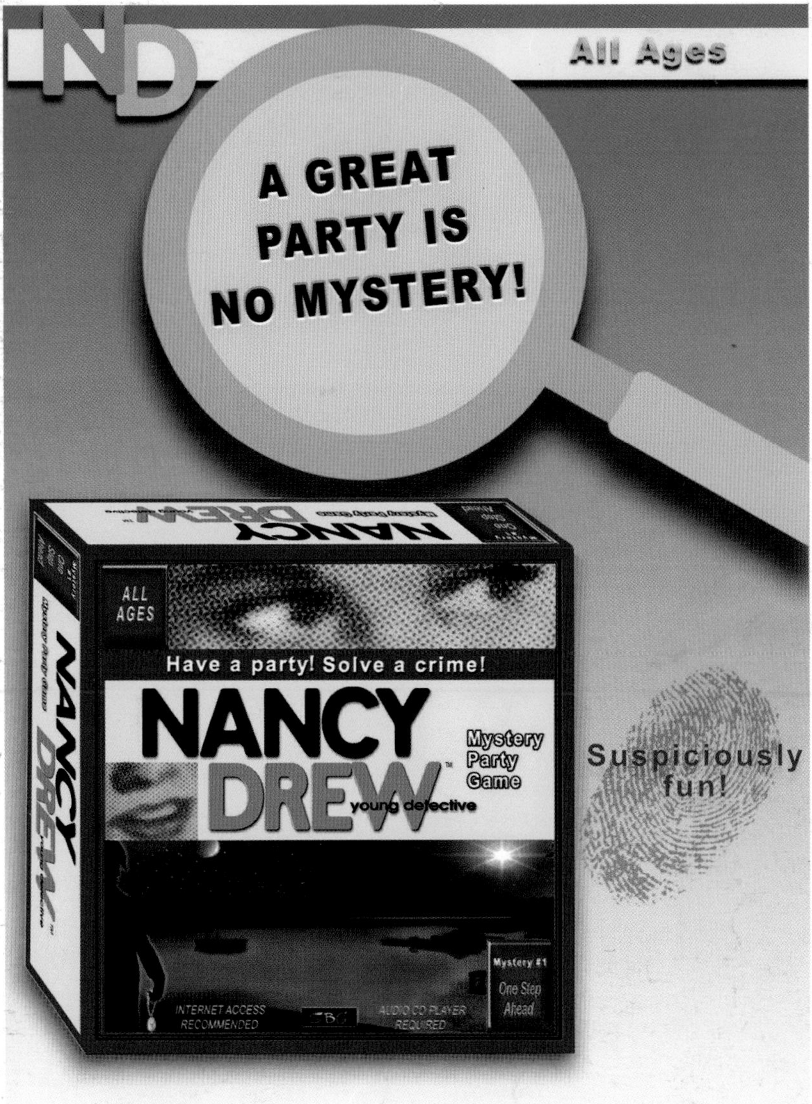

ND
All Ages
A GREAT PARTY IS NO MYSTERY!
ALL AGES
Have a party! Solve a crime!
NANCY DREW™ young detective
Mystery Party Game
INTERNET ACCESS RECOMMENDED
SBG
AUDIO CD PLAYER REQUIRED
Mystery #1 One Step Ahead
Suspiciously fun!

Get a Clue!
Read
NANCY DREW
girl detective™

The paperback series that started it all.

Smarter
Cooler
Quicker
Hipper
Surer
Braver
Faster
Newer

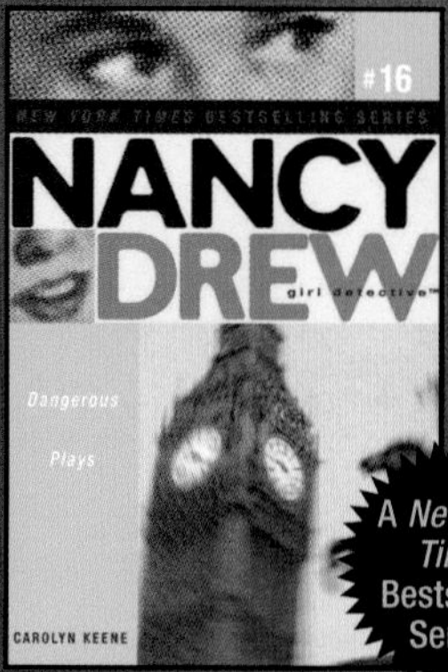

#16
NEW YORK TIMES BESTSELLING SERIES
NANCY
DREW
girl detective™
Dangerous
Plays
CAROLYN KEENE

A *New York Times* Bestselling Series!

Dangerous Plays
Available March 2006

In *Dangerous Plays*, crime calls in London! Nancy gets a phone call from Ned just before she flies out. Will she meet one of his professors for lunch before she goes? It seems some fishy things are happening at the professor's London townhouse, and he's hoping she'll check it out. Little does Nancy realize, though, that this simple task is only the beginning of a much bigger mystery . . . .

Have you solved all of Nancy's latest cases?

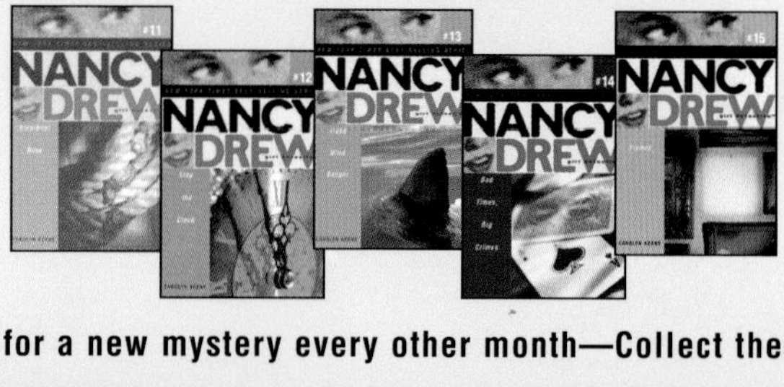

#11
NANCY
DREW
#12
NANCY
DREW
#13
NANCY
DREW
#14
NANCY
DREW
#15
NANCY
DREW

Look for a new mystery every other month—Collect them all!

Visit www.SimonSaysSleuth.com for more Nancy Drew

Aladdin Paperbacks • Simon & Schuster Children's Publishing • www.SimonSaysKids.com